WE — THE CONDEMNED

A band of legionnaires descends like vultures on the peaceful Arab village of Duaka and burns it to the ground — after brutally murdering a score of the men of the village, even as their weeping wives and children look on. Near the point of death, the Headman drags himself to Fort Valeau, to demand from his friend Captain Monclaire an explanation for the outrage. Fort Valeau is the only legion garrison for hundreds of miles, and Monclaire had given no such order. So who attacked the village — and why?

Books by John Robb
in the Linford Mystery Library:

JAILBREAK
NO GOLD FOR TINA
FOUR CORPSES IN A MILLION
THE LAST DESERTER
THE BIG HEIST
I SHALL AVENGE!

JOHN ROBB

WE — THE CONDEMNED

Complete and Unabridged

LINFORD
Leicester

First published in Great Britain

First Linford Edition
published 2014

A catalogue record for this book is available
from the British Library

ISBN 978–1–4448–2013–3

Published by
F. A. Thorpe (Publishing)
Anstey, Leicestershire

Set by Words & Graphics Ltd.
Anstey, Leicestershire
Printed and bound in Great Britain by
T. J. International Ltd., Padstow, Cornwall

This book is printed on acid-free paper

1

The Men of Peace

He came to them when the sun was going down. He was warped and made unlovely with suffering. His hands, once fine and slender, were now bloodied and repulsive because the nails had been pulled out of the fingers. His sensitive old face bore red weals where a hot branding iron had been pressed against it.

But Bala Aslaam, headman of the village of Duaka, was not yet defeated. He braced his wizened and senile frame as he came at last in sight of Fort Valeau. He tried to refuse the help of the legionnaires who came running to his assistance. But two of them lifted the Arab as though he were a child and carried him through the great, double gates of the fort.

He rested inside the guardroom for a few moments while a runner went to the office of the commanding officer. Then he

1

was rushed into the presence of Captain Monclaire.

Monclaire regarded him with a blending of sympathy and concern. He said: 'Aslaam, *mon ami*, you must go to the medical room at once . . . then you must tell me what has happened!'

Aslaam raised one of his hands. His voice was little more than a whispered croak.

'It would be no use . . . there is little time . . . some men know when their last hour has come, even as I know this is mine . . . '

'Then the medical officer will see you here.'

'No . . . if you please, I wish to speak with you alone . . . and it must be now . . . but I thank you, *capitaine*.'

Monclaire held a cup of water to his lips. Most of the warm liquid spilled down the Arab's matted and blood-flecked grey beard. But a little of it dribbled down his dry throat and temporarily revived his strength. His voice became slightly louder. He even attempted to sit upright in his chair.

And he said: '*Capitaine* . . . we have

been friends for many years, have we not?'

'We have, Aslaam. Ever since I first came to Morocco as a *sous* lieutenant.'

'Even so. And in those years have I not trusted the French and been their true friend?'

Monclaire nodded slowly, wondering.

The aged Arab's voice was reverting to a whisper as he added: 'But I now come to . . .'

Then his head rolled loosely and he began to slide from the chair. Monclaire put an arm under the thin shoulders and induced more water between the shrivelled lips. Again Aslaam revived.

Monclaire said, with a touch of anxious impatience: 'My dear Aslaam, all this can wait! You must let the medical officer attend to you. Your hands . . . your face, they . . .'

'Please, no. The minutes are departing quickly, even as my life can only endure for minutes . . . *Capitaine*, I came to ask you a question . . .'

'*Oui*, Aslaam.'

'My people at the village of Duaka are

3

peaceful, are they not?'

'They are peaceful, Aslaam. They are good people, like you, their headman.'

Aslaam summoned the last of his pitifully dwindling strength. He raised his tortured face and stared direct into the eyes of Monclaire. Then he said: 'If that be so, why have legionnaires burned down our village, *capitaine*? Why did they slay a score of our men? Aye, they were slain by legion rifles even as their weeping wives and children looked on . . . '

Monclaire had been holding the cup. He did not know that he had let it fall to the stone floor. He did not hear the crash of broken pottery.

After many moments he answered, in a voice that was almost as faint as the Arab's. 'Aslaam . . . you say this — this has happened to your people at Duaka?'

'Yes, and but two nights ago. They fell upon us like vultures on a suckling goat. I, the headman, was lashed to the ground, and in the sight of my people they did this to me . . . '

He gestured with his ruined hands towards his tortured face, and added:

4

'They thought I would die . . . but I had to live . . . to live long enough to ask you why this has happened to my innocent people . . . ?'

Monclaire stared down at the fragments of the cup. Unthinkingly, he ground them small with the toe of his boot. He was trying to achieve order out of the chaos of his mind.

Duaka . . .

It lay about forty miles south-east of Fort Valeau. Because of a surrounding belt of artesian wells the land there had a certain sparse fertility. Thus the hundred or so villagers were able to practise an elementary form of cattle-raising, and they occasionally bartered their surplus products with passing trade caravans. Duaka was more fortunately situated than most Arab habitations.

And it lay well within the administrative area of Fort Valeau. In other words, it was Monclaire's responsibility to protect the people there.

Monclaire did not need to consult his trooping schedule to know that none of his patrols had been near the village for several weeks. The place was usually visited once in every three months — as a routine check. The last such visit, he recalled, was about two months ago.

Monclaire said, gently, 'Aslaam . . . there is a mistake, my friend. There must be a mistake. I do not doubt that some people have attacked your village and murdered many of the men — and I pledge that they shall be brought to justice. But they could not be legionnaires. This is the only legion garrison for hundreds of miles. I gave no such order — it is unthinkable. And no one else could have done so.'

Aslaam began to breathe deeply and noisily. And now it was an effort for him to speak at all.

He croaked: 'Yea, you would not stain your hands with such treachery. But this I swear before Allah — they were legionnaires who slew my people and left Duaka a place of smoke and tears.'

'Aslaam — you, you are sure of this?'

'Have I not eyes to see? And those who were spared saw the legionnaires, too. They . . . they call for vengeance against you, my friend . . . they spat upon me

6

when I tried to tell them that you were not such a man. And when I said I was going to Fort Valeau to speak with you, none would come with me. They even refused to allow me a horse to ride. They said it was better that I go out into the desert and die there, rather than be tortured again by the legionnaires. But I did not die in the desert because above all things I wanted to speak with you, *capitaine*, and . . . and to ask you why this has been done to my people . . . and which officer ordered it to be done . . . '

His voice was fading to inaudibility. The fevered breathing became faster and yet more rasping. Monclaire rang the handbell on his desk. The orderly corporal entered. Monclaire said: 'My compliments to the medical officer. Ask him to come here at once and bring . . . '

He broke off. He followed the line of the corporal's startled gaze. Bala Aslaam was sliding slowly and silently to the floor.

Monclaire reached him in a single pace, but the Arab was already sprawled full length on the stone. Each breath was being taken with the desperate intensity of an exhausted athlete.

There was a tender quality about the way Monclaire cushioned the old Arab's head on his arm and, kneeling on one leg, said: 'Aslaam, I want you to know this . . . France does not murder her friends. I do not yet know why this has happened in your village, but I shall discover the truth and those responsible shall pay with their lives. That I swear to you.'

Aslaam's lips quivered as he tried to answer. But the cruel wounds and the long trek over the desert had taken final toll of his physical strength. Monclaire knew that the Arab's old fighting heart had endured too much.

But somehow Aslaam managed to raise one of his mauled hands. With it he touched Monclaire's face. And in the moment before death took it away, there was a hint of a smile in his eyes. The smile of a man who trusts his friend.

*　*　*

The daylight had almost faded when they removed Aslaam's body to the fort mortuary. Monclaire watched it being carried out on a field stretcher and he realized that he was incapable of emotion. It was as though part of him had died, too: the part that decided whether a man would weep or laugh. It was not only the fact of Aslaam's death that made him feel thus. It was also the circumstances of his death — and the fantastic story he had told.

When he was alone again, Monclaire sat on the corner of his steel desk and lit a cigarette. He wanted to think — think carefully. He had often impressed on junior officers that the first step towards solving a problem was to get a clear picture of the problem itself. 'Far too often,' he would tell them, 'we find officers trying to extricate themselves from some tactical dilemma without taking the trouble to understand the full details of that dilemma. That is the road to disaster. Comprehend the question first — then often the answer is simple . . . '

Bien! So now he must take his own advice. First, the matter of Aslaam himself. What manner of man was he? That, Monclaire told himself, was scarcely a question at all. Aslaam was typical of the best type of Bormone Arab. He was completely truthful. In all other respects he was trustworthy. He was intelligent enough to recognize the vast benefits French protection gave to his race and, in return, he had always given complete loyalty. His village of Duaka, remote though it was, had always been a model of a well-ordered Arab community.

Therefore, Aslaam must genuinely have believed that legionnaires had despoiled his village and murdered twenty of the inhabitants. That *some people* had done this was beyond reasonable doubt. The crux of the problem lay in Aslaam's belief that legionnaires had done so. He said he had seen them. All the others had seen them, too . . .

But they could *not* be legionnaires.

Monclaire put a match to the brass oil lamp that hung from the low ceiling. It shed a gloomy and somewhat inadequate glow over a large-scale wall map. He jabbed at various points on the map with his pencil. Here they were at Fort Valeau — six days' march from their advance base at Dini Sadazi. Here, three hundred miles to the south, was Fort Ney. And here, rather more than two hundred miles south-south-west, was the Arab trading town of Opono. There was a small legion garrison there. That completed the trooping arrangements within the brigade area.

And what did those dispositions show? They showed clearly enough that, except for his own garrison, there were no legionnaires anywhere near Duaka.

He sighed. He was about to return to his desk when another name on the map caught his eye.

Tutana . . .

It lay about a hundred miles from Duaka. It was one of the maintenance points for the new oil lines which stretched over thousands of miles of jungle and desert to the naval base at Oran. At one time there had been a threat of sabotage to those oil lines by Touareg tribesmen, but that had been settled during a terrible forty-eight hours in Dini Sadazi. And recently all troops had been withdrawn from that area.

But had he not read something about a desert road being built which would ultimately link Tutana with Oran? Monclaire unlocked a desk drawer. He pulled out a thick file of typed paper. Each sheet was headed: *Legion Etrangere. Operational Orders*.

These orders were issued by the High Command at Algiers. And in Monclaire's view they were issued on an over-generous scale. Sometimes three or four would come crackling over the radio in a single week and it was the duty of the unhappy cipher clerk to decode the Morse signs and then type the result into plain French. Like most garrison officers, Monclaire had a strictly unorthodox system of dealing with this spate of paper matter. He glanced at the subject headings to each paragraph. If they concerned him, he read on. If — as was usually the case — they did not, he read no further.

He had compromised between the two systems when — some weeks before — he had seen a paragraph headed 'Tutana-Oran Road'. He had perused it very quickly and without much interest. The High Command often announced plans for new roads.

Monclaire thumbed through the sheets. He found the one he wanted. He re-read it — this time with care.

The first part was an elementary treatise on the advantages of quick lines of communication. It was the sort of puerile humbug which staff officers regularly inflicted on their juniors. Then — reluctantly getting down to facts — the paragraph stated that work on the road was being started immediately at Tutana by the Fourth Zephyr Battalion.

A Zephyr battalion . . .

In other words, a punishment battalion. So there *were* other troops in the vicinity of Duaka. Troops who were not part of the normal garrison schedule. There was nothing unusual about the fact that the troops were Zephyrs. Building roads was their normal work. But . . .

But it could have some bearing on the attack on Duaka.

Monclaire's brow clouded as he thought about the Zephyrs. They were the dregs of the legion — hooligans who could not be managed by ordinary disciplinary methods. Usually they were arrant cowards on active service, and blustering bullies in the barracks room. Men who would knife a comrade for the sake of a few francs, or assault a wretched Arab woman in a back alley.

Monclaire knew that many civilians had the idea that legionnaires were sent to the Zephyrs for trivial offences. But it was a mistaken opinion and a gross injustice to the legion. It was only with the greatest reluctance that any legionnaire was thus condemned — and only after all other methods had been tried.

In some respects, legion discipline was harsher than that of other armies. It had to be — the officers and NCOs were contending with the clashing and simmering emotions of many differing races. And the men, too, were often cruder and tougher than other soldiers. But no self-respecting army wanted thugs in its ranks. And when the legion found them they were segregated to the Zephyrs, doing purely manual work.

Monclaire stubbed out his cigarette.

The orderly corporal reappeared. He put a cipher slip on the desk.

'Just received from Sadazi, *mon capitaine*.'

Monclaire breathed a gentle oath. The message was startling. It ran:

From: Commandant's secretary, Dini Sadazi. To: Officer Commanding, Fort Valeau. *Zephyr battalion of four hundred men mutinied at Tutana on 5th of this month. All officers and NCOs believed murdered. Mutineers in complete control of area and armed. They threaten to destroy oil installations if any attack is made on them. They announced this in a radio signal. Take precautionary action and report results.*

Four hundred men! Four hundred of the dregs of the legion free to do as they wished. Monclaire's mouth became dry as he considered the implications. The Zephyrs were trained soldiers and they would be completely desperate. Obviously, murder was of no importance to them. They had killed their officers. But — but what about the civilians who were living at Tutana? The oil maintenance engineers . . .

'Never,' Monclaire told himself, 'has

15

there been anything so terrible as this.'

And there never had. Zephyrs had mutinied in the past. But they had been comparatively small-scale insurrections, never involving more than twenty or thirty men. And they had been dealt with easily.

But four hundred! And in a remote area.

To deal with the situation, Monclaire had a garrison of one hundred and twenty-two officers and men. He could not detach more than half of them from the fort. But even if he'd had ten times the number, he would still be helpless, for a direct attack was impossible while the Zephyrs threatened to destroy the oil lines at the sight of a legion column.

Monclaire glanced at his desk calendar. The mutiny had occurred about a week ago. So it seemed that the Zephyrs had taken time to organize.

Then, with fantastic bravado, they had given the facts to Sadazi. Why? Because they believed that the best way of ensuring immunity from attack was to tell the legion of their threat to the oil. That, Monclaire decided, was obvious. Destruction of the oil pipes would be a matter of international importance.

And suddenly Monclaire realized that the raid on Duaka was no longer a baffling mystery. A party of Zephyrs must have set out on a looting expedition. That prosperous little village would be lush prey. The murdering and the torture would be an additional entertainment. But why would they want to loot, since they must have captured large supplies at Tutana? That was puzzling. But Monclaire no longer doubted that it was the Zephyrs who had attacked the village.

It was likely that other Arab villages would be attacked, too — with more sadistic killings. And the result? That would be measured in terms of hate. A great wave of Arab hate against the legion and France. And who could blame the Arabs? No one. They could not be expected to make fine judicial distinctions between scum and soldiers. Not when both wore legion uniforms.

Automatically, Monclaire's logical mind turned to possible lines of action. What was the enemy's weak spot? Ah, *oui*, that was simple. Their weak spot would be that party of looters. There were not likely to be many of them. So — the first move must be to locate them, engage them, and capture some of them. From the prisoners it would be possible to get more precise information about the position in Tutana.

Monclaire found a cipher pad. He thought for a moment, then he scribbled a message for Sadazi. It was brief — he did not want to commit himself too far at this stage. It read: *Signal acknowledged. Am making reconnaissance.*

The corporal took the message. As he turned to leave, Monclaire said to him: 'My compliments to lieutenant Gina — I wish to see him immediately.'

★   ★   ★

Lieutenant Gina adjusted the piece of plain brown paper which concealed the cover of the book he was reading. Then he lowered himself into the only chair in his tiny bunk and proceeded to concentrate intently on the pages of small type. And as he did so, a feeling of inner peace

18

pervaded him. It was a piece of magnificent good fortune that he had chanced to see this volume in a second-hand shop during his last leave in Algiers. These written words were giving him a new outlook on life.

Gina had only one peculiarity: he enjoyed his periods of duty at Fort Valeau. In the fort, he was second in command. He was a person of importance. In larger places he was a person of no importance. So he had a unique affection for the remote monotony of the fort.

Yes, that was his peculiarity. But in all else Gina was the Ordinary Man. He was no fool, but he was not particularly bright. He was no coward, but neither was he outstandingly brave. His appearance was not unpleasant, but it was not attractive either. He was not tall or short. He was not fat and he was not thin. He was a humanised negative quantity. His was one of the faces in the middle if the crowd. He was the sort of fellow that people met and promptly forgot.

And Gina knew this. It was his secret shame.

He longed for a powerful personality. It was, he often told himself, ridiculous that he should feel like a schoolboy in the presence of Monclaire, and like an idiot when trying to deal with that monstrous Russian, Sergeant Zatov.

Now it seemed that his dreams were to be realized. As he read avidly, the plain brown paper slipped from the book. It revealed a multi-coloured picture of a man with a massive jaw and fierce eyes. For some unexplained reason, streaks of forked lightning were emanating from his skull.

Under this portrait were the words: *How to be a Leader of Men . . . The Secrets Revealed by Professor Karlo.*

Any doubts which Gina may have felt about Professor Karlo's qualifications were quickly dispersed as chapter followed chapter. Gina had been fascinated by a detailed exposition on the Five Focal Points of Human Personality. Then he had moved on to a section dealing with The Power of the Mind. Now, after the preliminary survey, Gina was wallowing in the cream of the work. The professor was showing exactly how dynamic men reacted to every conceivable situation. For Gina, a new dawn was breaking.

Then the corporal arrived. Gina was annoyed when he heard the heavy boots approaching along the corridor, and then the knock on his door. He put the book down on his bed and said: '*Entre*'.

The corporal saluted. '*Le capitain's* compliments. He wants to speak to you, *mon officier.*'

Gina permitted himself a sigh. This, he decided, was really too bad. It was clearly understood that he had twelve continuous hours off duty every other day. He had two hours of rest left. Still, Monclaire was not the sort of commanding officer who deliberately made life unpleasant.

'Very well.'

Gina rose from the chair and went to a wall peg for his cap and sword belt. As he was putting them on, he realized that the corporal was still in the room. He had not, as one would have expected, saluted again, and promptly departed. Gina turned to find the reason. He was surprised to note that the NCO was staring with a sort of bovine amusement at the bed.

Dieu! It was the book. The plain paper had fallen away and it lay with the cover upwards. Now — now the whole fort would hear about it. The wretched fellow would be bound to spread the story that lieutenant Gina was reading how to be a leader of men. Gina made a wild gesture towards the volume. Then he said, accusingly: 'I — I found this in the corridor, corporal. Does it belong to any of the NCOs?'

'No, *mon officier.*'

'I thought one of them might be studying it with a view to promotion.'

'No, *mon officier.*'

'I've just been glancing at it. It's rather interesting.'

'Yes, *mon officier.*'

Gina suddenly realized that he had broken into a sticky sweat and was blushing like an adolescent. Damn it, couldn't that blasted corporal say something more than yes and no? And although the fellow was standing respectfully to attention, he now had a distinctly odd expression on his stupid face. It was a sort of flickering half-smile.

It was there, yet it wasn't there. Gina breathed hard.

'Very well — dismissed.'

The corporal saluted. It was a very correct salute. But the corners of his mouth were twitching very slightly. He turned about, and before leaving his eyes swivelled again towards the lurid book on the bed.

When he had gone Gina pulled a handkerchief from his cuff and mopped his face. He knew he was near to tears — tears of bitter humiliation. All young officers had to go through the process of being deflated by NCOs. But never — surely never in all the history of the legion — had a lieutenant been found in such a vulnerable position.

And what when Sergeant Zatov heard about it? Gina gave an involuntary whimper. The prospect was ghastly. That huge, red-bearded Russian had no mercy. And he also, in many subtle ways, made it clear that he had very little respect for Lieutenant Gina. As the senior NCO of the garrison, Zatov lost no opportunity to demonstrate Gina's lack of experience.

He dominated Gina — as he seemed to dominate most men except Monclaire. It was not merely a matter of his physical size. Zatov, a man with a wild temper, had himself been an officer in the Russian army. He had the assurance which experience gives.

Gina admitted to himself that he was afraid of Sergeant Zatov. His mere presence made him feel like a half-witted oaf. One look at the Russian's savage eyes and flaming beard reduced him to pulp. And the damnable thing was that he had bought the book with the very special idea of learning how to turn the tables on Zatov. He had wanted to surprise all the others, too, of course. But Zatov in particular . . .

Lieutenant Gina stumbled out of his bunk and headed miserably for Monclaire's office.

*　*　*

Captain Monclaire paused halfway through his story. 'Are you listening, Gina?' he asked.

'Er — ah, *oui*. Most certainly.'

'I'm glad, because you don't look as if you are very interested. As I was saying, I will myself take a detachment of fifty men to find these looters. The operation ought not to take more than two or three days, and I hope to return with prisoners. In the meantime, of course, you will command the rest of the garrison here. You will have Sergeant Zatov to assist you . . .'

★ ★ ★

Sergeant Zatov stamped into the legionnaires' mess room. He was gripping a long sheet of paper as though it were a seditious document. He glared down the two long lines of iron beds, some of which men were sleeping on. Then he glared at the table in the centre of the big room where a few legionnaires were playing cards under an oil lamp.

A black void suddenly appeared in the upper part of his red beard. Out of the void there came a voice of shattering volume. '*Gare a vous!*'

The card players dropped their pasteboards and jumped to attention. Those who had been asleep found themselves blasted back to the world of reality. Subconsciously, they stumbled to their feet. Zatov stared through the semi-gloom at each individual, as though probing their innermost secrets. Always a man of explosive temperament, he was now in a particularly vile mood. A wave of respectful apprehension passed down the lines of rigid men.

Zatov consulted the sheet of paper with distaste. He obviously considered it an unsatisfactory document. 'These legionnaires,' he announced, 'to parade in medium marching order at six hours tomorrow. Purpose: To engage and capture mutineers from a Zephyr battalion . . . '

He read out fifty names. Then, following a military formality, he asked: 'Any questions?'

The facts of the Zephyr mutiny were now well-known throughout the fort, having been recounted many times by the orderly corporal and the fort's wireless operator. Zatov knew this. Therefore he did not expect that questions would be asked. In any case, he did not want them. And he tried to suggest as much by his demeanour.

But a clipped voice came from a fair-haired legionnaire by the table. It spoke the peculiar French of the average well-educated Englishman. '*Oui, mon sergeant*. Who is leading the operation?'

Zatov fixed his eyes on Legionnaire Havers. And, as always, Pete Havers returned the glare with a casual indifference. Although Zatov would never have admitted it, he liked this Englishman whose personality was so different from his own. He liked the fact that Legionnaire Pete Havers was one of the very few men whom he could never intimidate. He was fascinated by the Englishman's cynical calm, which concealed a first-class brain. He was fascinated, too, by the fact that both of them had something important in common. Just as he had once been an officer, so had Legionnaire Havers. Havers had been a lieutenant in a famous British county regiment until a short prison sentence for manslaughter had ended his career. A killing, but far from accidental, had also ended Zatov's earlier career.

Zatov said, more quietly: 'Captain

Mondaire himself.'

'And will you be going, too, *mon sergeant*?'

Zatov — who had a liking for emphatic drama — pressed a huge hand to his enormous chest. He prefaced his answer with a series of Ukrainian oaths. Then: 'It has been decided that I — I, Sergeant Zatov — shall stay here in the fort as nursemaid to a gibbering suckling . . . '

It was very wrong of Zatov to make such an obvious and derogatory reference to a commissioned officer. But the Russian had little respect for the formalities of life. And he was glad that he could give vocal expression to his indignation.

'I say it is an insult,' he continued, his voice rising again to its normal volume. 'An insult to me and to my rank! Am I not a good soldier . . . ?' At this point there was a rumble of respectful assurance from the more timid of the legionnaires. 'Do I not serve France as well as any man in this garrison? Why, then, must I roost here with a military chicken while fifty of you march out to seek action against the Zephyrs? Why, I ask you? *Why?*'

He finished on a note of personal accusation, as if the legionnaires were in some way responsible for the injustice. Like many Russians, Zatov enjoyed working himself into a fury before an audience. But his indignation was genuine enough. And Pete realized this. He coughed discreetly. Then he said: 'But, *mon sergeant* — since Captain Monclaire is leading the party himself, he could scarcely take you with him.'

'Is that so, *mon legionnaire*? And why?'

'Because he could not leave the fort in the sole charge of the . . . the military chick.'

Zatov ceased to pull at his beard. He began to pat it gently, as if it had suddenly been restored to favour. He was looking almost benevolently at Legionnaire Havers. It was a transformation typical of his mercurial temperament. 'That,' he observed slowly, 'is very true. Very, very true.' He paused to reflect. Then he added: 'But I wish I were in your place, Legionnaire Havers. You are one of the fifty . . . Very well . . . *repos!*'

The men relaxed to the at-ease position.

Zatov turned to a large square of cork material that hung on the wall behind him. It served as a noticeboard for garrison orders. He pinned the paper to it. That done, he again confronted the legionnaires. He opened the void in his beard. Obviously he had something more to say.

But Zatov did not say it. Before the first syllable could be produced, another sound trembled on the air.

It was a long and wailing scream.

It was not loud — it came from far beyond the fort walls. But that scream contained within it all the satanic terror of the darkest ages. It was the unlovely music of human fear.

And it came from a woman.

2

The Day of Shame

There were a few moments of paralyzed silence, in which all the men in that mess room remained still and staring into space. It was broken by the sound of a single rifle shot from the ramparts — just one exploding cartridge. The harsh crack echoed against the fort's red sandstone walls. It was still echoing when the alarm bell clanged over the guardroom.

The result was automatic. It had been rehearsed scores of times in emergency drills. Each legionnaire rushed to his bed where a tunic and leather equipment were hanging. They were dragged on in a matter of seconds. Then rifles were grabbed out of the stands at the side of the beds. Each man then paused to push a charger of seven rounds into his Lebel, snap closed the cut-off, and check the catch to the safety position.

The bell was still sounding when the ninety men emerged from the mess room and paraded in treble file in the dark compound outside. Night duty at Fort Valeau — as at most legion forts — involved no more than a quarter of the total garrison strength at any one time. Thus, when the alarm had sounded, only about thirty legionnaires were on guard. Of these, eight were on the forty-foot-high ramparts — two sentries to each wall. The twenty-two others, including a couple of junior NCOs, were at 'secondary readiness' in the guardroom, which was situated immediately inside the main gates.

Twelve of the men at 'secondary readiness' ran up the steps to the ramparts, thus immediately increasing the rampart guard to five legionnaires for each quarter. The others formed a single line facing the gates. Zatov took command of the others. To the newly trained men, Zatov seemed to have become slow. To them, there was something exasperatingly deliberate about the way he insisted on the ninety legionnaires numbering off — *une . . . deux . . . trois, quatre . . .* Right through the ranks. And he gave the succeeding orders with meticulous care too. He even insisted on a left turn being done twice because the first movement was not smart enough.

To the uninitiated, Zatov seemed to be playing the fool at a time of emergency. But he was not. With all his faults — with all his bullying, with all his posturing and eloquent dramatising — Sergeant Zatov was a soldier. And he was also a natural psychologist. He knew that whatever happened, he must not appear to be flurried. *He* must not appear to be at all concerned. Under these conditions, a flustered NCO would produce flustered men. Zatov knew exactly what he was doing when he insisted on normal parade ground efficiency. And the experienced legionnaires, including Pete Havers, realized the fact.

At last, the vital order came: '*Avant!*'

They peeled off by sections for the four ramparts. Pete's section was detailed for the west ramparts on the left of the gates. The bell suddenly ceased clanging as the first of the line reached the base of the steps. Against the comparative silence, their boots made a tight clattering on the stonework. Pete was sweating and breathing fast when he reached the top and took up his position. So were all the others.

It was a relief for him to lay his long-muzzled Lebel on the firing groove and kneel behind it, staring out into the desert. At first, there did not seem to be much to stare at. A half-moon was riding high, shedding a reluctant glow of silver on the red sand, the rocks, and the folding dunes. They appeared to stretch and fade into lonely eternity as they had always done. And, now that all the ramparts were manned and all the legionnaires still, the only sound was the whispering of the restless night breeze as it fondled the dead wastes.

Pete glanced at the man next to him. He made out the tall and lean figure of Legionnaire Rex Tyle, the impulsive character from Brooklyn, New York. Pete whispered to him: 'I rather thought something was happening outside, but it all seems peaceful enough. Almost respectable, in fact.'

'There wasn't nothing respectable about that yell we heard.'

'Quite. But who was it? I thought it

came from this side and it certainly sounded like a woman.'

'It *was* a woman, bud. But if . . . '

The words died in his throat, as those of Sergeant Zatov had died.

The scream came again.

But this time it was not from far off. It was close and loud. It came from somewhere directly in front of them, from some invisible source in the night. Like the quivering call of a tormented ghost. Pete felt a stab of heat in his belly.

From far below in the compound Pete heard Monclaire's voice. He was talking to Lieutenant Gina and Sergeant Zatov. That was apparent by Zatov's deep-toned acknowledgments and Gina's thin and nervous ones. Presently, Monclaire mounted the west rampart with Zatov. Gina could be heard tramping to the opposite side.

The commanding officer and the NCO stood within a few yards of Pete. Monclaire had his field glasses up, trying unsuccessfully to penetrate the gloom. He clicked his tongue in annoyance, then nodded to Zatov.

Zatov was holding a long pistol of

unusual design. The barrel was wide and fluted. The breech was massive — almost as thick as that of an anti-tank rifle. He aimed it upright and slightly forward. When he squeezed the trigger the explosion was surprisingly faint. It was followed by a prolonged hiss, like that of an ascending rocket. At almost the same moment other explosions and hissing sounds were heard from the north, south, and west ramparts. Simultaneously, and with startling abruptness, the desert was bathed in an intense white light as the magnesium flare cartridges burst into silver balls and floated slowly down.

At first, Pete had to shield his eyes against the violently contrasting light. Then he saw her. An involuntary confusion of voices told him that the others had seen her, too. She was about a hundred yards beyond the wall.

She was a white woman. She seemed to be only partly clothed. Cruel crimson streaks stood out on her pale skin. And she was lashed by her arms and legs to the bare back of a crazed horse.

There are times when men are forced beyond the capacity for astonishment. This was so of most of the garrison. It was so of Monclaire. Of Zatov. And of Pete. They did not, at that moment, question the extraordinary manifestation; they merely reacted to it.

Monclaire glanced towards the other ramparts. After a brief pause, a series of long whistle blasts came from each of them, signalling that nothing had been observed there. He muttered to Zatov. The sergeant looked to his left and saw Pete. He said: 'You come with me, legionnaire. It seems a lady is in distress, eh?' He laughed richly. There was no great sense of chivalry in Zatov's makeup. He handed his flare pistol to a corporal. Then, with Pete following, they clattered down the stone steps.

The flares were fading as they reached the gates. But, as the great lateral bar was being raised and the gates swung open, four more cartridges hissed into the velvet sky. Pete and Zatov hesitated just outside the walls. Because they were now on a lower level, they had temporarily lost sight of the rearing horse and its terrified burden.

Zatov, whose eyes were used to many thousands of desert nights, saw them first. He pointed slightly to their right. The horse, its fear accentuated by the flares, was running in wild circles. But it was gradually moving away from the fort. 'The lady doesn't want to meet us, eh?' Zatov said, and laughed again. The situation, chilling to Pete, was obviously amusing to Zatov, who added: 'We'll have to shoot the horse . . . ' He raised his Lebel. Pete was about to restrain him, but Monclaire's voice came from the ramparts.

'Sergeant! Do not shoot unless you have to! You may kill the woman.'

Zatov turned and looked upward. 'But *capitaine*, the range . . . it is not much. I will not miss the horse.'

The voice, now rasping, came back from the elevated shadow. 'Do not argue, sergeant. Even if your aim is good, the horse may fall on the woman and crush her.'

Zatov cursed comprehensively but quietly, and lowered his rifle. He muttered to Pete: 'So we are not allowed to shoot! Then what are we to do? That horse is frightened and it will run off if we try to approach it. Does the captain think that we can overtake it? Or does he expect us to sing to it, so it will stand still and listen?'

Pete ignored Zatov's rhetorical questioning. He noted that the flares were again fading and he said: '*Mon sergeant* . . . I think it's the flares that are frightening the animal. It would be better if we tried to manage without them.'

Zatov spat viciously, then nodded. He turned again towards the shadow on the ramparts and repeated Pete's suggestion. Monclaire answered immediately. '*Mais oui*. There will be no more flares unless you ask for them. Take your time. If you want any more men to help let me know, but I think the fewer the better.'

Pete fully agreed. A large number of legionnaires would certainly have scared the horse away for good. The last flare spluttered out and the horse was no longer visible. But when they last glimpsed it, it was about two hundred yards off and trotting in tight circles that were taking it due west.

Pete felt the cool wind on his face. He realized that it was a factor in their favour. He said to Zatov: 'The animal's probably tired, and now the flares have stopped it'll rest. If we move quietly we ought to be able to get up to it — it won't be able to scent us because the wind's in the wrong direction for that.'

Zatov scratched his beard. He was becoming intolerably bored with the entire business. He had expected some sort of military action. He had certainly not anticipated chasing a horse round the desert. And he had little concern for the woman. He had already decided that she was probably one of the white camp followers who attached themselves to the Arabs. There were many such females who began their dubious careers on the waterfront at Algiers and ended it in some remote part of the Sahara when they no longer pleased their masters.

In short, Zatov was more than willing to dissociate himself from the operation.

He saw his chance. Glancing down at his huge thighs and giant-sized boots he repeated: 'Move quietly, legionnaire? Me! But I am not a quiet man!'

Pete admitted to himself that this was true. Sergeant Zatov had many military accomplishments, but stealth was certainly not one of them. He had only one mode of approach — he marched. He marched with feet stamping and arms swinging. So Pete began: 'If I may suggest it, *mon sergeant* . . .'

'Suggest anything! Suggest that we make neighing noises! Suggest that we make a secret approach by burrowing underground, if you wish . . . I, Sergeant Zatov, am annoyed!' He spat again, to emphasise the point.

Pete smiled. Then he continued: 'Perhaps it would be best if you stayed here, *mon sergeant*, and I approached the horse alone.'

Zatov made a broad gesture. 'It is admirable! Do just that — it is an order!'

Pete slackened the sling on his Lebel and slung it across his shoulders. Then he moved towards the place where he had last observed the animal. He moved slowly, deliberately, and after covering a hundred paces he stopped to listen. At first he could hear nothing — nothing except that eternal nocturne of the breeze in the sand. Then, faintly, his straining ears detected the sound he was hoping for. It was the sonorous breathing of an exhausted horse. It was directly in front of him.

Pete's progress became even slower. Minutes — long minutes burdened with tension — elapsed before he saw the animal again. It seemed to emerge suddenly out of the darkness as a black and narrow hulk. And on its back he discerned the silhouette of the woman. The white haze of her flesh was very still. Pete wondered: 'Is she dead? I don't want her to be dead. I want to know who she is . . . where she came from . . . how she got out here . . . '

The answer that Zatov had automatically accepted made no appeal to Pete. An instinct told him that this woman — even though he had not yet seen her properly — was no white slut, no wharfside wretch who had tagged herself onto a band of Arabs. And he was surprised to find that, even as he had been conjecturing, he had drawn level with the animal. It was still unaware of his presence. Pete resisted a temptation to look more closely at the woman. He glided another step forward until he was just behind the horse's head.

Then he conceived a silent curse. There was no bridle on it. Not even a halter. Nothing by which it could be secured, unless he grabbed the ropes which bound the woman. But that might be disastrous. The only place to control a nervous horse was at its head. If he tried to hold the rope that ran round the base of its neck he would certainly be thrown clear when the animal reared. And it *would* rear. Its sweating, twitching hide showed that it was both excited and exhausted.

There was only one way. First he would have to calm the beast, then release the woman.

It was still munching at a clump of cactus, still ignorant of the man who stood beside it. Pete stretched out his left hand. Deliberately, he laid it on the woman's arm. Her skin was silk. At last, he found himself gazing full at her. Her face was towards him. Her hair, honey blonde and long, was mixed with the coarse black of the horse's mane. There was a weird pallor about her features — delicate and lovely features. Her mouth, small and full, was twisted down at the corners, a reflection of suffering. Her eyes were closed. Only the faint but regular movement of her small breasts showed that she lived. The slim body was partly covered by the remnants of a white silk dress, and there were weals on her shoulders. They showed fierce and red through the tears in the fabric.

Pete moved his hand until it covered hers. It was a calculated manoeuvre. The horse was accustomed to the pressure of her hand — he wanted to replace it with the pressure of his own. Very gently, he pushed his fingers under her damp palm and stroked the animal. It went on eating.

Pete groped for his bayonet. He pulled it from the scabbard by painful inches and held it close to the horse's neck — to be used if it took panic. Then he whispered to it. They were the universal words of men who understand horses. Its ears pricked up. It raised its head and trembled. Pete went on whispering and stroking — but with the bayonet still ready. Then he eased forward and patted its neck. It did not move. He stood in front of its foam-flecked mouth. It showed the whites of its eyes — and backed away a pace.

Pete did not attempt to follow it. Instead, he took off his kepi and filled it from his water bottle. He put it on the ground. The horse came forward and drank eagerly. But most of the liquid was seeping through the material and into the sand. Pete refilled it and corked the now empty bottle.

Now there was little danger of the horse bolting. He could release the woman. He pulled a knife from his capote pocket and cut the ropes. She rolled into his arms. She was surprisingly small and light. It was like holding a child. He kneeled with her across his knee and pushed the hair from her eyes. The lids, with their contrasting black lashes, flickered slightly. Then they opened suddenly and Pete was looking into twin circles of deep brown.

He tried to smile at her, but it was not a convincing attempt. She was staring at him with an expression of both fear and relief. When Pete drew in a breath to speak he found himself hesitating. What was her nationality? Which language would she understand?

Because of her vivid fairness, it was unlikely that she belonged to any of the Latin races. But she could be one of any of a dozen other European peoples.

The problem was solved for him. She whispered in a dry, croaking way: 'This . . . this is the fort . . . ?'

It was the slightly nasal and not unattractive New York accent that Pete heard spoken every day by Rex. At first he was too surprised to answer. Then he said: 'You're just outside Fort Valeau. You're all right now . . . You've nothing to worry about. But . . . who are you? How did you come to be roped to the horse?'

The two questions came with a rush

that could not be restrained. She did not answer them. But the fear was fading from her face. And she said, still whispering: 'Water . . . I want water, please . . . '

Pete looked at his empty water bottle. And at his kepi, which the horse was licking. He felt stupid. 'You'll be looked after in the fort,' he said lamely. 'I haven't any water left.'

'Then hurry — please hurry!' There was an unexpected strength in her voice. Pete put an arm under her tortured shoulders and the other under her legs. She winced with pain as he stood up, but her eyes never left him. 'You . . . you're English?' He nodded. 'That's kind of nice . . . but for God's sake . . . get me in the fort.' She twisted her blonde head around, as if expecting to see something in the night. Something that symbolised terror.

Pete followed her gaze. He could see nothing except the thinly illuminated dunes and the distant black mass of shadow that was Fort Valeau. He looked again at the horse. It was still licking his sodden kepi. He bent down awkwardly and replaced the cap on his head. The wetness made him shiver. He felt the involuntary movement of his body against hers. He knew a primeval surge of desire. It was a long, long time since he had seen a woman such as this. But to be actually holding her, to know the suggestions of her flesh, was almost intolerable.

He said: 'You're frightened — why?' And as he spoke, he was surprised by the callous crudity of his own words. There was a gruff, animal harshness about them. He felt a tinge of shame. He thought: 'Hell . . . that's what living without women does to men . . . living in that ghastly fort . . . it makes us beasts . . . ' Then he realized that she had not answered his question. He saw why. Her eyes were closed again, her limbs completely relaxed. She had floated back into unconsciousness. And he knew a new emotion — frustration. Now he would have to carry her to those grim walls.

Perhaps he would never talk to her again. She would never tell him why it was that she had been found alone and tied to a horse. He would never hear from

48

her own lips who she was and what she feared. For all such information he, Pete Havers, would have to rely on wild and fickle rumour. But he wanted to know about her. He wanted the truth. He had a right to the truth, he told himself fiercely. Had he not saved her?

Pete felt a revulsion against his humble rank. Against the vile stroke of fate that had deprived him of the status and authority of the Queen's commission in the British Army. And he envied Monclaire, who occupied much the same position that Legionnaire Pete Havers had once held. He stood for a full minute, holding her close, his skin drawn tight over his cheekbones and his mouth twitching. The injustice of it! It would take about three minutes to carry her to the fort. For just three minutes she would depend upon him. Then, once they were within those gates, he would lose her. She would be taken out of his arms. She would be carried into the medical officer's room. Then she would be interviewed by Monclaire . . . And she would tell Monclaire all about herself. Monclaire would know and

Monclaire would probably offer her wine. They would dine together in the officers' mess . . .

In those moments, Pete almost hated the man whom he normally liked; almost held in contempt the officer he respected. All because of the lovely creature he held in his arms. Because, through a basic instinct, he did not want to give her up to any man.

It was the glitter of gold under the moon that restored his mental balance, which cooled his passion. It reflected from a finger on her left hand. A wedding ring. It confirmed his instinctive feeling that she was no desert tramp. Women who attached themselves promiscuously to Arabs did not wear the conventional sign of matrimony.

So she had a husband. Or, perhaps, she had once had a husband. But who was she? And he saw again the red weals on her shoulders. They could have been caused by a stick or a whip. A whip! Against this small, delicate creature! He felt sick because the thought affronted a funda-mental conception of human dignity.

Pete did not realize it, but at that moment the last remnants of his desires faded. He was again his normal, clear-thinking and slightly cynical self. She needed proper care — and she needed it urgently. He cleared his throat, intending to call for Sergeant Zatov. But he changed his mind; for if he called, Sergeant Zatov would come running towards them. And they would no longer be alone.

He would walk quietly to the fort — thus they would be together just that little time longer. As he carried her towards the great and grim walls, the moon went behind a cloud. And he was glad, because the absolute darkness made their loneliness complete. And Zatov did not see them until they were almost upon him.

3

Fiends of Tutana

The medical officer said: 'She is exhausted and badly bruised, but she is not seriously harmed. I don't think it would be wise to question her until morning.'

Monclaire clicked his tongue. 'What's she doing now?'

'Sleeping. I have given her a sedative.'

'Very well. Let me know immediately she is able to talk.'

The medical officer saluted and went out. Monclaire sent for Lieutenant Gina and said to him: 'I'll have to delay the operation against the Zephyr band for a few hours. And the longer I wait the more likely it is that they will attack more villages. Or they may even be on their way back to join the main body of mutineers at Tutana. But I can't very well leave until I have spoken to this woman. I must find out who she is and what's happened to her.'

Gina said diffidently: 'Do you think it might be the work of the Zephyrs — the woman, I mean?'

'It's very possible. Who can say? But I know this — I don't like having a woman in the fort. It is bad for morale.'

Gina tried to give a worldly-wise nod, suggesting that he very well knew why. Then he said: 'I suppose we'll have to escort her to Sadazi.'

'*Mon Dieu, non*! That's the trouble. With the Zephyrs terrorising the area, I cannot spare an escort. Anyway, not at the moment. As soon as I have spoken to the woman I'm going to radio a request for a plane to fly out here from Oran to pick her up. But I have not much hope of that being done, unless she is a very important person, which I doubt. Only the biggest planes can make the return trip and none may be available immediately.'

Gina brightened considerably. Like most very young men, he imagined that he had an irresistible fascination for women, though his past experiences did little to confirm that belief. So Gina's imagination darted to the hypothetical future. He foresaw the time when Monclaire had left the fort and he, Gina, was in command. The lady would be his personal charge. His guest, in fact. He would entertain her in the mess. He would be suave. He would be witty. And all the time he would suggest through his demeanour that he was a modest yet gallant person . . .

Rumour said that the woman was beautiful . . .

The adolescent romantic in Gina was detecting vast and fruitful possibilities. And Monclaire? He was disliking very intensely the prospect of leaving a young woman in his fort. True, he expected to be absent for no more than a few days. But much could happen in that time. Monclaire had seen her when she was brought into the fort. He had given her no more than a cursory glance after noting that she was unconscious. And he had given a few gruff instructions to the medical officer. But he was not entirely indifferent about her. He disliked admitting it — even to himself — but he was touched by her supreme beauty. It seemed to him that, whatever her story may be, she would need the advice and reassurance that only a man of poise and maturity could offer.

It was an odd train of thought for the normally precise Monclaire. Those who knew him would be dumbfounded to learn that there was anything of the sentimental romantic in him. But then, Monclaire, too, was a Frenchman . . .

Monclaire was the first to awake from the reverie. He glared at Gina. 'Well?' he asked curtly. 'Well? Have you any more absurd suggestions to offer? If not, I think you ought to cease bothering about the woman. It — er — it interferes with the correct discharge of your duty . . . '

Gina coloured munificently. '*Mais capitaine!* I was not bothering about her,' he lied.

Monclaire snorted. He stretched forward on his desk and drew a file towards him. 'It was clear upon your face,' he said as a parting shot. 'You cannot deceive me. Your attitude towards her must be strictly correct. That is an order. In any case, you are far too young to be thinking about women.'

Gina paused at the door. He turned desperately towards the captain. 'But she is young, too,' he said.

★ ★ ★

And in a bleak, stone-walled room, usually reserved for sick officers, Rene D'Aplis lay in a drugged sleep. But she was not entirely at rest. Sometimes her lips would part and she would mumble an incomprehensible word or phrase. There were occasions when she twisted and turned between the blankets as though under torment.

The medical officer who came in to look at her observed these symptoms. 'She is dreaming,' he said to himself, and went away.

Rene D'Aplis was indeed dreaming — of heaven and hell. Each scene pressed itself on her fevered mind in a way that was unreal, yet too real. It was like watching characters perform through a thin curtain. Like hearing people talk through deep amplifiers. And like seeing yourself move towards a disaster which you know is there, but which you are powerless to avoid. Powerless, because it is all really more than a dream. It is a weird repetition of the facts . . .

The heaven.

When she lived in a small but good rooming house near Brooklyn's Concord Street.

Each morning except on Sundays she crossed Manhattan Bridge on her way to the public library off Times Square. She had been working there as an index clerk when the party of French engineers were being shown round. Many such official parties visited the library, and comprised all nationalities. This was just another of them.

Until she was asked to demonstrate the index system. A dark, good-looking young Frenchman had asked her to do it. And he was smiling gently as he asked. The demonstration took quite a time and neither of them worried about the fact that the rest of the party had moved on. It was in the nature of things that Andre

D'Aplis should ask her out to dinner that evening. And equally natural that she should accept.

The French engineers remained in New York for five more days. And she and Andre met on each of them — always going to the same small, intimate restaurant. Then he was away for a month, visiting other parts of the States. But there was a letter from him each day, and she posted one each day before crossing the bridge. Andre was three thousand miles away when he asked her to marry him. He was in Los Angeles. The cable ran to exactly sixty-three words, and therefore cost quite a sum of money. Rene's answer was not so expensive. Just one word.

They were married by the French consul in New York. Two days later they sailed together for France. Andre's home was at Toulon, the seaport on the Mediterranean, where he was employed on research connected with the fuelling of warships. They lived there for two years — happy.

The hell.

He said to her one evening: '*Cheri*, I am being sent to a place called Tutana.' She had felt a coldness take her heart, like a single gust of wind before a storm.

'Tutana? Where is that?'

'In Morocco. It's very lonely and very small. Just an Arab settlement really, and a thousand miles from almost anywhere. But the main junction of the new oil line is there and quite a few maintenance engineers have to go out. I'm one of them.'

She said: 'You mean we are two of them. I'm no engineer, but I'm with you.'

He had argued. He would only be away a year, he said. And it was no place for a woman. But, because he had really wanted her to go, he had in the end agreed.

She had never told him so, but she had hated Tutana. Hated the hot and glaring remoteness of the place. Hated the mean little prefabricated buildings in which they and the other French families lived. Hated the eternal stink of oil, which seemed to seep out of the pipes and pumping towers. Hated the same faces seen at the same time each day. But, because she was with

Andre, it had been tolerable. Until the ordinary legion garrison was withdrawn from the place, and the Zephyrs took over.

She had said to him: 'Why have the legionnaires gone?'

He had been pouring himself a glass of wine. He was tired after the day's work. Suddenly he also looked worried. 'They say there's no need for them now,' he told her. 'At one time it looked as if there might be trouble with the Touareg Arabs, but I hear that the garrison at Dini Sadazi, under an officer called Monclaire, has broken their power.'

She remembered the Zephyrs, who had marched that afternoon. She had watched them from the veranda of their tiny home, and she had been frightened. They were in Legion uniform, but they did not look like legionnaires. They looked like men apart from other men. She had searched face after face with mounting anxiety, looking for something: a trace of sensitivity, a suggestion of ordinary human feeling. But she saw only brutes: big brutes, small brutes, sullen brutes, arrogant brutes. It was as if — which was indeed the case

— they were a cross-section of the darkest depths of mankind.

Except, perhaps, for just one of them.

He marched near the front of the long column. He was not at all big, either in height or width. In fact, in comparison to most of the others he was almost dwarf-like. And his huge head gave a hint of deformity. It seemed too vast a thing to place on such a body.

But it was his features that captured her attention. There was vast strength in them — but not strength alone. His nose and his mouth were big, but they were finely, almost delicately formed. His forehead, so far as it could be seen under his kepi, was high and broad, suggesting mental power. And his eyes . . . They were absorbing, demanding, terrifying eyes. Then was the light and the shade of madness in them. Of genius too.

Those eyes had rested on hers as he marched past. She had felt herself hypnotised by them, as though captivated by an evil. And he had smiled at her before turning his head at the command of an NCO. It was like the Devil smiling.

She asked Andre: 'Why have they sent the Zephyri here?'

He told her it was to build the new road.

She hesitated, then said: 'They frighten me a little.'

He had laughed. 'You've no need to worry. They are well guarded and as the road progresses they will move away from Tutana.'

Then she had told him about the little man, the man who had frightened her more even than the others. He recognised her description.

'I was told about him only an hour ago,' he said. 'One of the officers of the Zephyr battalion was saying that he was a strange and dangerous man. They have to keep a special watch on him. And you know, *cheri*, he was once a poet.'

'A poet!'

'*Ah oui*. His name is Pavani. He is an Italian.'

'But — how did a poet get into the legion? I didn't know they were fighting men.'

Andre smiled. 'You are making a great

mistake there. Some of the most valiant soldiers have been poets and artists. But this man Pavani, I do not know that he is valiant. But I do know that he was an anarchist in Italy. Everything he wrote encouraged anarchy and bloodshed. He fled the country when he was about to be arrested.'

'Then he joined the legion?'

'He did. He would not have been accepted if the recruiting authorities had known about his background, but they do not enquire too closely.'

'And then . . . ?'

'And then he caused trouble in his company. He is the sort of man that fools will follow. Several times he incited resistance to orders and he was punished. And once, when in Algiers, he wrote a lying article about conditions in the legion for an Italian newspaper. The paper did not publish the article. They returned it to his commanding officer, and Pavani was again punished. But still he did not go to the Zephyrs. A man has to be very bad before that happens.'

'Well — what did he do next?'

'He got drunk. He attacked his commandmg officer with a knife and nearly killed him. Pavani is lucky he was not executed. He is a fanatic, a bad man, but you will see no more of him . . . now, *cheri*, let us have supper . . . '

But she did see Pavani again. She saw him once when she was going to the oil line administration office. A detachment of *Tirailleurs Senegalais* had just escorted a camel train in with supplies and mail. Such visits only came every two months and they were a big event for the Europeans in Tutana, who crowded the office for letters and parcels from France. Pavani was marching with a dozen Zephyrs towards the roadhead.

Deliberately, she had tried not to look at the Zephyrs. Not because of contempt. It was because she hated to observe the misfortune of others — however well merited. But she had felt compelled to look. It was as if a magnetic and malevolent power was controlling her vision. And before their eyes met she knew he was there. He had a pick over his shoulder, but it did not bow him; he was marching erect. And he was smiling at her, just as he had smiled on that first day. And it had the same effect. But with one addition. This time, she recognized something else in those evil and brilliant eyes. It was something that all women recognize immediately in a man.

It was desire. Hot, furious, yet patient desire. The sort of passion that could wait and wait . . .

And he tried to speak to her. His words came in a soft, sibilant French with only a slightly over-Latinised accent. The sort of French that an erudite Italian would speak. Not the debased tongue which was the common verbal coinage of the legion.

'*Y a-t-il des lettres pour . . .* ' He had been making a polite enquiry about her mail. Polite, anyway, in the phrasing of the words. But a corporal of the guard interrupted him with a bawled reprimand. Then he was gone. *And Rene suddenly felt ill and weak. She felt helpless under a pall of wickedness.*

The mutiny came at six o'clock one morning. She awoke to hear a strange echoing against the metal walls of her home. At first she lay very still, trying to clear her head of sleep and wondering what it could be. Then she realized that Andre was out of bed and dressing. She called to him and he said: 'Stay where you are — I'll find out what's happening.'

He went out and was back in a few minutes. There was sweat on his face and it had become haggard. At first he did not speak. He went to his private drawer, unlocked it, and took out a heavy automatic pistol. Then he groped for a carton of cartridges, found it, and charged the magazine. She watched in silence. And she knew. Knew what was happening outside. When he had put the pistol into his pocket she said: 'It's the Zephyrs — isn't it?'

He put his hands on her shoulders. His grip hurt her. He said: '*Oui*, it is the Zephyrs. They have mutinied. It has been very well planned. They have seized the arsenal and they are all armed. Most of the guards are already dead . . . '

'Can't we radio for help? There's the wireless station.'

'They have captured that, too. And

help, *cheri*, is a long way off. The nearest is at Fort Valeau, and that is only a very little garrison. What could they do against hundreds of these fiends? And in any case, they could never get here in time to . . . to save us.'

She whispered: 'You mean we'll be killed? They'll do that to us? But we've done the Zephyrs no harm. We're civilians!'

As she spoke the sound of the shooting, which had died down for the moment, began again. This time it was very close and very loud. And mingled with it were the shouts of men giving orders, the thud of running feet, the screams and moans of the wounded.

She put her arms round Andre, clinging fiercely to him. Then she felt him take a hand away from her. She watched that hand of his go into his jacket pocket. When it came out it was holding the gun. It looked efficient and ugly in the thin morning light. She knew what he was going to do. Each word was like a ton weight as she said: 'You're going . . . going to use that?'

He nodded. His eyes were moist, but his mouth was set firm. 'It is better. You, you are the only young and beautiful woman here. If you fell into the hands of the Zephyrs they might not kill you immediately.' She understood. He added: 'It will be over quick, *cheri*. Then I will follow . . . '

But the bullet that killed Andre came shattering through the window. It was a stray, but it might have been aimed by an expert marksman. It entered the side of his head, just above the ear. Rene felt him slip through her arms to the floor. She was incapable of reaction. She stared down at him and at the gun, which was still in his lifeless hand. She was still staring when a mob of Zephyrs stormed into their home.

They formed a circle round her. They prodded her and pushed her. They uttered foul obscenities and roared their amusement. Then they tried to push her out of the room. But she did not want to leave. She wanted to stay with the huddled form that had been Andre. And she knew an erupting fury against those who had killed him. Without warning, she turned on her tormentors. Her fingers flashed out and the nails made deep scratches down the unshaven face of one brute. He howled with pain as the others laughed. Then he took hold of her and she was helpless in his grasp. She screamed under the storm of blows and she felt the agony of great bruises opening and contusing.

He might have killed her there and then if Pavani had not come in. She was only dimly aware of his presence. But she knew that the torture suddenly ceased and the mutineers went out — except Pavani. He carried her to a chair. He forced wine down her throat. Then he stood over her. And again she felt forced to meet the fanatical compulsion of his gaze. Compelled, also, to listen to the uncanny music of his voice.

'You will be harmed no more,' he said. 'We, the Zephyrs, now hold Tutana and the only law is my law. They will do as I say. And I say that you are mine . . . '

She whimpered and he put a hand under her chin. It was a surprisingly fine hand. It was calloused by unfitting toil, but it was still slender. 'You are mine,' he repeated. 'I always intended it to be so from the day I marched into Tutana. But you have nothing to fear. I can wait. I can wait until you accept me of your own free will. There are some things which cannot be taken by force and you are one of them . . . '

He kept his word. For days she had lived under guard, but unmolested, in her home. It had been like living in a morgue. She was the only one to survive the mutiny. All the other civilians, and all the NCOs and officers, had been massacred.

Then Pavani came back to her. He did not seem to notice that she cowered away from him. He said: 'We are going out into the desert, you and I and a few of my men.' She did not answer. He went on: 'The position here is secured and well organised. I can safely leave for a few days. I am radioing the French authorities to tell them what has happened. No, that is not surprising. They dare not interfere with us. If they were to do so we could blast the oil line so that it would take years to repair. Explosive charges have already been put beneath it for that purpose. You see, we are in a very strong position here. In fact, we are unassailable.'

She knew that the oil line was vital to the fuelling of the French fleet at far-off Oran. She knew, too, that the French would do — or refuse to do — almost anything to avoid its destruction. And it could be blown up in a moment, at the first suggestion of an attack on the Zephyrs.

It was then that she spoke to Pavani. It was the first time that she had done so. She said: 'But why are you doing all this? You cannot stay here for ever. Soon your supplies will run out and you will starve.'

He smiled and shook his huge head. 'We'll not starve. I, Pavani, do not plan things that way. In a week or two we will leave Tutana. We will march for the coast of Tripoli and there we will break up and disappear into the small towns. After that, it will be for each of us to make his own way back to Europe. Some may be recaptured, but not many. And we will be all right. I have made careful plans for us — for you and I.'

She put a shaking hand to her blonde head. She mumbled: 'You're mad! Crazy! You'd never make it. That march would take weeks. Legion forces would soon know about it and intercept you. Why don't you surrender now? Why don't you let me go? For God's sake let me go . . . '

He put up a hand for silence. And she became silent. 'You are right,' he said. 'In the ordinary way we would be intercepted before getting near the coast. But I am making arrangements for the legion to be kept very busy. That's why we are going into the desert.' She gazed at him blankly and he continued: 'We are going to raid a few Arab villages. We are going to kill a few of the inhabitants — yes, kill them, even as we killed the people here! The village Arabs are not very clever. They will not know exactly who we are or why we are doing it. They will only know we are legionnaires. And the old hatreds will soon burn bright again. The story of the atrocities will sweep through all Morocco and then — then the warriors will rise

72

again against the legion. Ah, yes — I know the legion will ultimately defeat the poor wretches. But it will take time. And the legion will be very occupied defending itself while we make our great march.'

Sick and frightened though she was, Rene recognized the ruthless possibilities of the plan. But only a madman could carry it out. It was elevating butchery to an exact science. She said: 'I think you are utterly without mercy.'

'I think I am,' he agreed smoothly. 'My philosophy — the belief to which I have dedicated my life — does not permit mercy. A true and natural state of humanity can only exist when all the artificial forces of law and order are destroyed, and to destroy them we have to kill. A great Russian called Bakunin and a Frenchman named Proudhon first expounded these tenets. I am merely a disciple.'

There was a terrible throbbing in her head. She knew he was prepared to enlarge on his anarchistic beliefs. She did not want to listen. She wanted to know about what was to happen to her. So she said: 'Why are you taking me into the desert? Do you think I want to see you massacre more innocent people?'

'I am taking you because, since I have decided to lead these operations in person, it would not be safe to leave you here. No one will dare harm you while I am near. I have absolute control, for the Zephyrs know that without my brain to guide them they would be helpless. But if I were to be many miles away . . . ' He gestured meaningfully.

She asked: 'Where — where are you going first?'

'To the village of Duaka. It is, I understand, a prosperous little place. And it is not far from Fort Valeau. When blood flows at Duaka, the garrison at the fort will have much to think about. Then other villages will follow. And you — you may not have an easy time. But that is all to the good. You are a woman of courage, but I shall see your courage break and your spirit bend under the hardships. And then . . . you will come to me . . . you will do so knowing that only I can make your life tolerable . . . ' Those eyes were fixed on her.

And she did something that she had never done before — which she could never have imagined herself doing. She spat at him. It was the one fundamental act of defiance that lay open to her. And her sudden ferocity expressed itself like the snarl of an enraged cat. 'You! Do you think anything would make me come to you, the man who helped to murder my husband! Listen to me — listen! Even if you were not a demented fiend, it would still be impossible for me to touch you. Your body is ugly and loathsome. Your mind is diseased. If I had seen you in France or in America without knowing anything about you, do you know what I would think about you? I would feel sorry. That's all! Just sorry for a deformed dwarf . . . '

Her courage and her venom vanished with her last words. Suddenly she was afraid again. His big face had drained of blood under its dark tan. His lips were trembling. He epitomised fury. She knew she had struck at his one vulnerable point — and she had been as ruthless as he. For a moment she thought that his slender hands were going to clutch her by the throat, for they were raised as if to do so. But, abruptly, his entire awkward body relaxed. He forced his mouth into his satanic smile.

'I am content to wait. Under hardship and humiliation you will break. You will come pleading to me. And on that day . . . on that day I shall write a sonnet in praise of you! Yes, a sonnet. A work that will stretch to the stars and be sweeter than anything composed by d'Arezzo or Wordsworth, or Keats. You shall see . . . ' He went away. And it was then that she knew beyond all chance of doubt that Pavani was mad.

And the next morning she was put on a horse. She protested when her legs and arms were lashed round the animal so that she was forced into an almost prostrate position. But Pavani said: 'The discomfort is intentional. But there is also another reason for securing you. You see, you have the only horse in Tutana. It belonged to our late commanding officer. The rest of us must travel on foot. So I have to be sure that you will not use the animal in any stupid attempt to escape me.'

There were thirty Zephyrs in the raiding party. And Pavani, who had put on an officer's uniform, had chosen them well. He had delved into his human cesspool and scraped for them. Following him, they were the ultimate in savagery. Yet he had absolute control over them. Their relationship was that of animals to a master.

She nearly died during the march to Duaka; nearly died of exhaustion and humiliation. The cruel sun afflicted her body, making the weals on her shoulders grow more red and more painful. The crude voices, the eternal absence of privacy, the unending insults, burned like splashes of acid in her mind.

They hobbled her horse and left her just outside the village when they raided Duaka. At first she had been able to see and hear nothing. But not for long. The single cry of a child had trembled in the night. It was followed by a clashing medley of shrieks and shouts. They were punctuated by the irregular sound of rifles.

She closed her eyes. She tried not to listen. But she had to listen . . .

The horse, already restless, was becoming frightened. It was pulling at the neck halter which secured it to a cactus tree. And it was that pulling which gave her the clue — the clue to escape. Her hands were also roped round the animal's neck, and the tips of her fingers made contact with the knot of the halter. Pavani would never have secured the animal like that. But Pavani had been too busy anticipating the raid to worry about securing her. He had left that to one of his moronic Zephyrs. But even the moron could not be entirely blamed. It was pure chance that the tugging of the horse had eased the knot into contact with her hands.

The untying of it was a long and desperate task. She could use only the tips of her fingers, but she managed it. At last, the rope fell away. And the animal became still, as if astonished by its own freedom. For a moment she had been baffled, too. It was like escaping from some prison and then not knowing where to go. But her doubts did not last for more than a few seconds. Pavani had said that the village was not far from a legion fort — Valeau. So perhaps the unguided animal might find its way there. Perhaps . . . it was a slender chance. But better, infinitely better, than enduring the Zephyrs. At worst, she could only die in the desert.

She kicked the animal's sides. It whinnied and trotted in a tight circle. Then, its ears flat, it trotted in a northerly direction and away from the carnage of Duaka.

It was night . . . it ran. Then it walked. Sometimes it stopped. It was day under the fury of the sun . . . the horse was exhausted. But, by some instinct, it found a water hole . . . She had to watch it drink . . . she could not reach to drink herself . . . It rested beside that water, now indifferent to its burden. Night again . . . and again she kicked the animal into movement . . . but it was reluctant . . . slow and heavy hoof thuds on the sand . . . and it seemed to be going in circles. Another day . . . but she could not remember any of it save the agony of thirst, mercifully relieved by periods of semi-coma.

And another night . . . She did not know it was night until she opened her eyes to realize that the horse was no longer moving slowly . . . it had forced itself into a sweating trot, as if sensing something . . . She saw direct in front, a mass of shadow . . . like a great giant resting . . . but this was no giant . . . walls . . . tall walls . . . the fort . . . it must be Fort Valeau . . . a miracle . . .

But the horse was turning away. Away from the fort, back into the hell of the desert. She screamed. Screamed because of the fear of it. And despite her swollen throat, he knew that the sound was loud and terrible. Then she heard something else — something that had become all too familiar: the report of a Lebel. Just one shot. And she knew that they must have heard her. It must be a sentry firing a warning. Now, from far off, the music of bells. No, just one bell. She screamed again. And she knew no more until she was being held in the strong arms of a legionnaire . . .

Rene had lived it. And now, in the fort's sickbay, she was looking up at

Captain Monclaire. She saw a smallish man; a lean, dark man. He was smiling at her. She felt well enough and grateful enough to try to smile back.

He said, '*Madame*, I want to know who you are and what has happened.'

She told him. Told him everything, pausing only when she found difficulty in finding the apt French phrase. When at last she had finished, Monclaire's face reflected a strange blend of anger and sympathy.

He said: 'Madame D'Aplis, I am sorry. It was the task of the legion to protect you, your husband and the others. I fear the legion has failed. But you personally have nothing more to fear . . . ' He hesitated, and then added: 'I suppose you will want to get back to France as soon as possible.'

She was sitting up against two hard military pillows. She nodded. Then she shook her head. 'Well — not exactly France, captain. I'm an American, remember. I want to get back there. There's nothing to keep me in these parts now that — that . . . '

'I understand. I will do everything

possible. But I'm afraid it will take time. Our nearest base is Dini Sadayi, which is six days' travel. You will appreciate that I cannot spare an escort at the moment. In the meantime, please think of yourself as our guest.'

In his office Monclaire was able to think. He threw his cap and cane on the desk, dropped into the chair and sighed. Then he lit a cigarette and addressed his mind to the problem.

Problem? *Mais non*, it had the makings of a disaster.

The oil line was in the hands of several hundred mutineers. That had already been clear. And it was serious enough. But what he had not known was the fact that the mutineers had prepared a careful and practical plan for a mass escape. And they were setting the desert alight in order to achieve it! The horror of Duaka was to be repeated, perhaps several times. And each separate and deliberate atrocity would produce an ever-increasing hatred in the Arab world against all things French. And while the legion forces were grappling with the chaos, the Zephyrs would be moving undisturbed towards the Tripoli coast and freedom. Therefore, his original plan to go out into the desert in an effort to make contact with the small group of mutineers had become more imperative than ever. If he could prevent more villages from being attacked, then Pavani's entire operation might collapse.

And if Pavani himself could be killed or captured . . .

If that were to happen, the Zephyrs would be no better than a headless monster. There would be every prospect of starving them into submission in Tutana without endangering the oil lines. And if they attempted to march to the coast, they would be cut off and cut down. *Oui*, that was the answer! Somehow Pavani must be eliminated. And the time to do it was now — while he was moving about the desert accompanied by only some thirty of his men. If only that Zephyr group could be found . . .

There was the snag.

He glanced towards his large-scale wall map of French Morocco. Then he crossed towards it. The position of the fort was marked by a red circle. With his pencil, Monclaire sketched a square round the circle, embracing an area of about two hundred miles in each direction. It was within those limits that the Zephyr group was likely to make its next attack. But just where? Just how was he to find them? In the vast and trackless wastes it seemed an impossible task. They could appear almost anywhere without warning — and disappear within the hour, leaving behind a scene of slaughter and hate against the legion, whose uniform the Zephyrs wore.

Monclaire regarded the map carefully and sucked his pencil. '*Dieu!*' he told himself. 'I think I am frightened. If I make a mistake, if my judgment is wrong and I take my column to some place a hundred miles from the Zephyrs . . . the High Command would not excuse me. *Non*! They would not think of the difficulties. They would call me a fool. Perhaps I am vain, but I do not want to be thought a fool. I must not fail. I must reason this out . . . '

He proceeded to reason.

The mutineers had last been seen about forty miles south-east of the fort, at Duaka. He put his pencil on Duaka. To reach it, they had travelled a hundred miles from Tutana. The village had obviously been selected with the object of causing trouble in the immediate area of the fort. And there was no other legion garrison within a reasonable distance. Therefore . . . Duaka must be as far from their base as the mutineers intended to go. Logically, they would not make trouble on the outward journey. That could lead to complications, so far as they were concerned. They would first reach their maximum distance, and then ravage the villages on the way back. Therefore . . . The next point of attack must be at a place nearer Tutana. That eliminated exactly half of his square. But it still left an enormous amount of territory.

The mutineers, Monclaire reminded himself, were on foot. That automatically limited their mobility and the time they could remain in the desert — even allowing for the looting of Duaka. So they would scarcely move towards the fort, or due south, which would also increase the time needed to get back to base. Therefore . . . They must be returning along roughly the route by which they had arrived, taking the shortest way to Tutana.

Monclaire drew a line between Duaka and Tutana. It passed through or near four villages that were marked, and three smaller ones, which the cartographers had ignored. But Monclaire knew they were there. That left seven potential places for attack. Could the process of elimination be carried further? Monclaire thought that it could. One village was quite close to Tutana — a matter of sixteen miles. That would be an unlikely target since the Arabs there would probably know where the Zephyrs came from. Pavani would not want to risk Arab counter-raids on his own base. And the three minor villages could be ignored. They would not be worth Pavani's powder and shot.

So three were left.

Now the time factor had to be assessed. It was about sixty hours since the attack on Duaka. Monclaire realized that in that time at least one more village must have been ravaged, probably the one next to Duaka. 'I'll be hearing about it,' he muttered. 'I'll be hearing . . . ' Therefore . . . The obvious way of interesting the band was to make a forced march to the next village but one to Tutana, and wait there for the Zephyrs to arrive. The villa was named Hagal.

With a feeling of sickness, Monclaire realized this would mean leaving the other places to the mercy of Pavani. But, nevertheless, an Arab insurrection might be avoided. For the people of Hagal would see for themselves what had happened when his column engaged the Zephyrs. And the truth would soon spread.

So Hagal it was! A forced march there with fifty men — he wished he could spare himself more; a day or two of waiting, perhaps, then the action which would end in the capture or the death of Pavani and the crumbling of the great mutiny.

Monclaire sent for Lieutenant Gina. 'My column to parade in fifteen minutes,' he told him. 'Objective — the village of Hagal.'

4

Hell at Hagal

It had been an innocent enough village. In it, the women had woven baskets and rugs for barter with the passing caravans, and the men had tended a small herd of thin and despondent goats. They ate and they worked and they slept. And they raised children who would also eat and work and sleep. Therefore, in spite of simplicity, the Arab villagers had been fundamentally the same as all people in all parts of the earth.

But not now.

Now every man was dead. They lay sprawled between the mud hovels, their stiff faces still showing bewilderment and fear. The women were huddled in remote corners, still trying to comprehend the horror that had come to them that day. A few of them wept. But most were silent and dazed, like beaten animals. The children stood about in uneasy groups, staring at the bodies of the men who had been their fathers.

The fate of this village had been worse even than that of Duaka. It had paid for the fury of Pavani. And Pavani, as he led his Zephyrs away from the ruins, was still racked by his emotional tumult.

He had lost her! Lost her! Lost her!

The single stark fact kept repeating itself; hammering itself against the walls of his brain.

He had searched for her. Of course he had searched. But he had soon abandoned that as hopeless. Tracks left in the sand were soon covered, and in any case how could they, on foot, chase a horse?

Pavani had considered her likely fate. He was forced to admit the possibility of her reaching the fort. It was no great distance, and Arab horses had an instinct for finding places of habitation, just as they found water where a man would never do so. Certainly, the odds were that she would die with the animal amid the lonely sands. But those odds were not so great as might seem at first sight.

It was symbolic of Pavani that, despite his frustrated and surging passion, he retained his capacity for shrewd judgment and ingenious action. Both men would have been annoyed by the comparison, but it remained a fact that in that respect, Pavani had something in common with Captain Monclaire.

It was Pavani's genius, which, after the second raid, dictated that he should push on to Hagal without delay. And the woman — the woman who had escaped him — was the foundation of the decision. She certainly did not know just which villages he had intended to attack on his return journey. But she possessed a general outline of his plans. And *if* she got to the fort, she would be able to offer information from which an intelligent garrison commander could make deductions. And it occurred to Pavani that the commander at Valeau had a very high reputation indeed. That officer might realize that he, Pavani, could be intercepted. And he might also realize that Hagal was the natural place for such an interception . . .

So Pavani decided that there would be no more raids. The risk was too great. The two raids already carried out would have to suffice. He would march to Hagal with all possible speed, so that if a legion column was indeed coming, he would be there first. He would be there to receive them.

But he would not attempt to fight an orthodox military action against the column. Oh no! That would be the essence of stupidity. But, nonetheless, a most delectable shock would await the legionnaires if they came . . .

★   ★   ★

Pavani and his Zephyrs came within sight of Hagal four days after the raid on Duaka.

Monclaire's column sighted Hagal just thirty-six hours after the Zephyrs had moved in.

★   ★   ★

A carrion bird flapped above Hagal's hovels. Then it folded its shaggy wings and dropped out of sight. It was the only sign of life in the place.

But Monclaire continued to inspect the village carefully through his field glasses. It was difficult to get a clear view. The heat haze was the reason; it shimmered above the sand like a wall of steam. It always did at any time of the day except in the first light of morning. But Monclaire was satisfied with what he saw: it was obvious that the village had not yet been attacked. There was no sign of damage. In fact, the whole aspect of Hagal was that of a normal Arab village taking its rest in the heat of the afternoon.

He replaced his glasses in their leather case and said to the corporal: '*Bon*. We are in time. The place has not been touched. It is a great relief — I feared we might be too late.'

Corporal Offlan was a Latvian. He was also newly promoted and he earnestly desired to justify his commanding officer's apparent confidence in him. He tried to do so by attaching himself to Monclaire on every likely and unlikely occasion. He followed Monclaire with the devotion of a dog to an indifferent master. He repeated Monclaire's phrases, so that he had become a mobile echo.

'And *I* feared we might be too late,' Corporal Offlan said.

'We will move into the village, allay the doubts of the inhabitants, then wait and hope,' Monclaire said.

'Yes, we'll wait, and hope,' said Corporal Offlau.

Monclaire pursed his lips with annoyance. He was having serious doubts about Offlan. The man had passed through the corporals' school at Saida, in Algeria, with fair marks. Therefore he had been morally compelled to award him the red *galons* of a junior NCO. But he was finding the fellow distinctly tedious. It was only because he was new in his rank that Monclaire was showing patience with him. If he had known that Offlan had the characteristics of a parrot he would not have brought him as second in command. He had been guided by the fact that he believed in giving young N.C.O.s immediate responsibility. And because, since Gina was his only officer, he had thought it advisable to leave as many experienced NCOs as possible in the fort. For, whatever happened, the fort must remain secure.

Monclaire turned to his sweating and tired column. '*Avant!*' he barked.

Corporal Offlan, of course, barked, '*Avant*' too.

There was music in the movement of that column of fifty men: the crunch of boots on sand, the gurgling of water in steel bottles, the creaking of leather equipment. They all created a steady and not unpleasant rhythm. Pete, from his position in the centre of the second file from the front, found himself listening to it, as he had often listened. It made a soothing background to the fatigue and monotony of a desert march. And it made a change from thinking about Rene D'Aplis. He had thought a lot about her since the march for Hagal had started. Monclaire, who believed in giving his men background information, had recounted her story before they had left the fort.

But, as always, there were other sounds that spoiled the music of the march. A man in the file immediately behind Pete's was muttering to another about some injustice in a card game. 'He played an ace of diamonds . . . an ace! Ah yes, it was his all right. It came from his own private pack. It hadn't been dealt to him. How do I know? Because I was the dealer . . . '

Still further back, a Romanian was using his inadequate French to tell an allegedly funny story to a disinterested Greek. 'She said she wanted to marry him . . . *non*, that is wrong . . . I mean he said she wanted to marry her . . . I will begin again . . . '

And on Pete's right, Rex Tyle began talking. Rex was saying: 'It looks like the Arabs in that village sleep mighty heavy.'

At first Pete did not react to the comment. They were just words which mingled with many other words spoken along the column. Then, suddenly, the import of the sentence occurred to him. 'What do you mean? Do you expect to see them running about? If you do, you'll be disappointed. The Arabs always relax at this time of day.'

Rex used a single and highly lurid verb.

Then he said: 'I know quite a bit about the Arabs myself, bud. And right now I'd be expecting them to wake up and come running out to meet us.'

Pete looked curiously towards Hagal. It was getting quite close now — less than half a mile away. And there was no sign of activity. No sign of any human being. It did seem curious! Even the somnolent villagers must by now be aware that a column was approaching. And since Arabs were naturally a curious race, they would in the ordinary way be showing great interest. Hagal was not a place which the legion visited often. Certainly not often enough to make the inhabitants indifferent.

Then a solution occurred to Pete. He laughed and said: 'I don't wonder that the Arabs are staying put. They're probably scared out of their wits. They've likely heard by now of what happened at Duaka and they'll be wondering whether we're going to give them the same treatment.'

Rex considered. 'I'm not so sure,' he said. 'If they were scared, I guess they'd beat it — not wait to be murdered.'

'Not necessarily. People don't quit their homes all that easily. They'll be waiting to get a closer look at us first.'

Monclaire had been reasoning on the same lines as Pete. And so the column trudged on, nearer and nearer to the silent village, until they were less than three hundred yards from the nearest mud hovels and the rancid stink of the place was already tainting the air.

Then Arabs emerged from behind those hovels. They emerged suddenly, as if in obedience to an order. They numbered about a hundred: probably the entire adult male population of Hagal. Some of them carried cumbersome muskets of ancient design. Others had scimitars. A few were armed only with short stabbing knives.

They charged in an ungainly mass at the column. Those with the muskets fired from the hip as they ran, and the column — still marching — wavered in several places as hot ball shot tore into the ranks.

Monclaire acted by instinct. His lifetime of military training took over when his normal senses were numbed with astonishment. 'Arreter!' The legionnaires stumbled to a halt. 'A boite!' The files peeled off, forming themselves into a rough square. There was no time for numbering and similar exactitudes. '*Gare . . .* '

Sweating hands tugged at rifle slings, pulling the weapons from the shoulders where they had been hanging. Safety catches were pushed free. The legionnaires peered along the leaf sights at the advancing mob. The entire operation had taken under thirty seconds, but in that time the Arabs had halved the distance between them.

It was now that Monclaire hesitated. And even as he did so, he cursed himself for his own timidity. Should he fire at them — or over them? If a volley over their heads did not deter the Arabs, there would not be time to fire again. But he did not want to kill, if killing was unnecessary. For these were not Arab warriors; they were ordinary village folk. And they must have been seized by some mass madness, since they were obviously bent on slaughter. At least half a dozen of the legionnaires had been hit by that ragged fusillade from the muskets.

What was he to do? At them or over them? Over them or at them? The questions flashed through his mind in a few brief seconds. But they were seconds of mental torture.

Then he made his decision.

He ordered the facing rank to fire over their heads. He did it because he was fundamentally a humane man. It was a mistake. But it was a mistake occasioned only by his humanity. The simultaneous crash of the Lebels was like the momentary rattling of sheet iron. Thin wisps of cordite smoke drifted across the square. And the Arabs checked their rush — but not for long. They looked about them, searching for casualties. And, finding none, they gave a screeching yell and flung themselves over the last few yards which divided them from the legionnaires. Desperate fingers whipped back the Lebel bolts, extracting the empty cartridge cases. The bolts were pushed forward again, then slammed down.

But it was too late. Too late to take a sighting for a volley that would rip into the wall of Arabs. For the Arabs were upon them with their muskets and their scimitars and their knives.

Pete had been in the facing file that had fired the useless volley, and was now taking the first impact of the charge. A young Arab — he was more a boy than a man — knocked aside Pete's Lebel and attempted to stab him with a short knife. It was a wild movement, the blade describing a wide downward curve. Even amid the chaos, Pete had no difficulty in stepping back. The Arab lost balance and sprawled at his feet, the knife falling from his hand. Instinctively, Pete aimed the Lebel down and took first pressure on the trigger.

Then he stopped.

The boy was staring upwards and at him. His narrow chest was heaving, and one thin arm was flung across his body as a futile shield. Pete thought: 'Hell — I can't kill kids . . . ' Then the thought was knocked out of his head as another Arab — older and stronger this time — aimed a crushing blow at him with the stock of a musket. Pete ducked and as the wood passed over his head he fired at the man's chest. The Arab ran backwards for several yards as though smote by a battering ram. When he fell, a pink froth was bubbling out of a three-inch cavern in his lungs.

In such close-quarter work, Monclaire had an advantage: he had his automatic pistol, which was far more easily used than a Lebel. But only once did he shoot to kill. That was when he found an arm encircling his neck from behind, and glimpsed a knife plunging for his ribs. Like most smallish men, Monclaire was deceptively strong and agile. He twisted round like a snake and, as he twisted, he fired. The slug slapped into the centre of a brown face, which suddenly became a crimson face. He felt the point of the knife penetrate his tunic and prick his skin before it dropped to the sand.

On the other occasions, when his life was not in such imminent danger, Monclaire fired only to disable. He knew that, although they were heavily outnumbered, the legionnaires would eventually beat off the attack. This rabble would not be able to break a square of battle-hardened soldiers. And he was still reluctant to cause casualties among Arabs who for years had been perfectly peaceful. There was some reason for this senseless attack . . . some misconceived motive for which these primitive people could not be held responsible.

Monclaire's confidence in the outcome of the engagement was justified. It ended in less than two minutes; two minutes in which men scuffled and panted, cursed and moaned. Minutes in which blue uniforms and grey-white robes swayed and heaved together like a pile of maggots on a heap. Then, at one side of the square, the Arabs broke away and stumbled towards the village. They did so with that weird precision which often characterizes a spontaneous decision to retreat.

The others followed. But it was not a rout. The Arabs of Hagal still held onto their swords, knives and muskets. And when they reached the hovels they stopped, they turned, and again they faced the legion square, but this time at a more discreet distance.

Monclaire made a swift survey. The attack had cost him some twenty casualties, of which seven were dead. The Arabs had left more than a dozen lifeless bodies behind. Most of the wounds inflicted on the legionnaires were trivial, but two of them were not. One man, hit in the preliminary fusillade, had received a ball shot in his stomach. The other had a fractured spine where a blade had cut into it. Monclaire knew — they all knew — that the entire resources of medical science could not save them. But the entire resources were not, in any case, available. All that was to hand in the way of medical skill and treatment lay in the person of an orderly who carried a first-aid kit. The kit, slung over his shoulder, contained bandages, splints, and a bottle of pain-relieving tablets. The tablets had been administered to the two men. But they continued to sob, retch, and curse. Their eyes were the eyes of men who were approaching death slowly, but who wanted to reach it quickly.

Monclaire gazed at them thoughtfully, deliberately suppressing any emotion. He looked at the group of legionnaires huddled round the dying men, trying to offer words and gestures of comfort. It was no time for sentiment. No time for ethical debate. There were times, Monclaire reminded himself, when mercy took strange forms. This was one of them. That which he was about to do had been done a thousand times before on a thousand battlefields.

The legionnaires turned away while he fired his pistol twice.

The crack of the second kindly explosion died away. Then it seemed to repeat itself. And repeat again and again in a great chattering of lethal noise. There was a twanging in the air around their heads. Men in the square were clutching at their faces, their throats, their bodies, then falling to the sand, making the red grains redder still.

Monclaire swiung round and faced the village. Then he saw why the Arabs had attacked. And he saw who was attacking now. A line of about thirty-nine in legion uniform had emerged from behind the hovels. They were kneeling, and each had a Lebel at his shoulder. In the middle was a small, grotesque and fanatical-looking fiend in ill-fitting officer's clothes.

The Zephyrs! They had been waiting in Hagal!

Monclaire felt fear and guilt clutching at his heart. *Dieu . . . ah, mon Dieu . . .* it was clear now! Those fiends! They must have come to the village representing themselves as a regular legion force, and told the Arabs that the Zephyrs were on their way. The Arabs, the poor cheated imbeciles, had believed them! And they had attacked the column, believing that they were defending their homes . . . Believing that his, Monclaire's, column were the Zephyrs . . .

It was so simple!

Taken absolutely by surprise, the square disintegrated like fragments of a shell. Pavani's mutineers released three rounds rapidly at them in twice as many seconds without reply. And there could be no effective reply. As he flung himself flat, Monclaire knew that already he must have lost more than three-quarters of his men, and they would all be dead within a few minutes. Against such odds they had less than no chance. And, in all probability, the High Command would never be sure of just what had happened at Hagal.

The handful of survivors were attempting to find cover where there was no cover to find. They were doomed men. All of them. Another few rounds would finish the last of them.

But those last few rounds did not come.

Instead, Monclaire heard a sibilant voice. It was calling in almost perfect French. And it came from the little man who must be Pavani. He was saying: 'You may surrender, *capitaine*. It would be sensible to surrender. It would be suicide to refuse.'

Monclaire raised his head from the sand. He looked about him, at the dead and the dying, and at the few dazed and bewildered men who still lived. There was the Englishman . . . he had survived, although he was wounded . . . and the American . . . Corporal Offlan, too. Offlan was already crawling to his side . . . curse Offlan!

In all, he had an effective strength of eight men. Eight men! Where, seconds before, there had been more than forty! He had no option on the question of surrender. There was no possible point in continuing to resist. A certain type of civilian, fed on the synthetic heroics of the film studios, might think that he ought to fight on to the last man. But no soldier would hold that opinion. Soldiers fought to achieve a purpose, and if the purpose became impossible to achieve they stopped fighting. When, as sometimes happened, they did fight to the last man, there was always a good and logical reason for doing so. Monclaire knew that no such conditions applied now. If he continued to resist, his eight men would be wiped out in a few seconds.

But if he surrendered and they lived, there *might* be a chance of getting information back. Monclaire rose to his feet and faced the line of Zephyrs across the short stretch of sand. His eyes met those of Pavani and he felt a mild sense of shock. He suddenly realized that the man who confronted him was more than a fanatic, more than any mere mutineer. Pavani was also a great leader. A man with a massive brain, which was made more dangerous because it was horribly warped.

'We are coming to you,' Monclaire said.

Pavani laughed. 'You are wise, *capitaine*. Tell your men to leave their rifles on the ground. And you, *capitaine*, will have no further need for your pistol. Please drop it.'

Slowly, Monclaire unknotted the lanyard and let the hot pistol fall at his feet. He had to wait before he could give the orders to his men. There was a tightness in his throat which made speech almost impossible.

And as the eight unarmed legionnaires stumbled forward, Monclaire thought: 'I have been outwitted, I have been outmanoeuvred! *Dieu!* It seems that Pavani the Zephyr is a cleverer man than I . . . '

5

This is Justice

'You will be roped together,' Pavani said. 'Then you will come with us to Tutana. If we march through the night we ought to be there by dawn.'

Monclaire tried to protest. 'There is no reason to tie us up like slaves,' he said. 'We cannot escape.'

'But you are slaves,' Pavani purred. 'Your status has undergone a considerable change, *capitaine*. I intend that you shall be constantly reminded of that fact.' He nodded to one of his Zephyrs, a leering, slab-faced fellow whose body stank. The Zephyr came up with a coil of hemp line. Monclaire's wrists were lashed behind his back, then the rope was carried back to Pete, who was similarly secured. Then Rex and the others. It seemed that they were to move in single file with about a yard's distance between each man.

Pete had a tugging pain in his right shoulder. A Lebel bullet had passed over it, grazing the bone and leaving a mess of torn skin and flesh. The bleeding had almost stopped and the wound was not serious, but it needed bandaging. All wounds needed immediate bandaging in the heat of Morocco. Already, flies were buzzing round the congealing blood; and because his hands were secured, Pete could no longer brush them away.

Monclaire noticed this. 'This legionnaire must have a field dressing on his wound,' he said.

Pavani made an indefinite gesture. 'This is not a hospital, *capitaine*.'

'I am aware of that. But the wound must be covered. If it is not he will suffer agony from the flies.'

'I am deeply moved, *capitaine*. But I intend that he shall suffer. His agony will not compare with the agony I and my comrades have experienced in our Zephyr battalion. But I intend that in due time you will all know what suffering is. That, *capitaine*, will happen when we reach Tutana. This is justice, is it not?'

Monclaire ignored the question. He was looking at Pete. And he said to him: 'The night will soon be here, then the flies will have gone. Have courage, *mon ami*.'

Pete managed to smile. He knew the torture his open wound would cause before darkness brought relief. But somehow the prospect seemed less awful after Monclaire's words. Monclaire, the captain, had addressed him as *mon ami*! My friend! And they disseminated a feeling of comradeship along the file. Pete was not alone in experiencing a strengthening of the spirit. All eight of them felt it. For the barriers of rank were down. The captain, whom they had liked from a distance, was now among them and of them. Monclaire was a good psychologist. He knew exactly when and how to use the touch of informality. And he had the personality to make a couple of words appear vastly important and encouraging.

Meanwhile, there was a pathetic activity in and outside the village. All the inhabitants had now emerged. Some of them were dragging back the bodies of those Arabs who had been killed. The others were chattering and gesticulating towards the captives. Pavani watched them for a while. He seemed to be thinking as he stroked his big and bristled face. Then he turned again to Monclaire. He was smiling. He often smiled, but it was never a pleasant spectacle.

He said: '*Capitaine* . . . it seems that you are not very popular with the Arabs. That is natural. They imagine that you and your men are Zephyr mutineers — and, therefore, are responsible for the deaths among their people.'

'I have guessed that,' Monclaire said, and he turned away.

'But,' Pavani continued slowly, 'I am now faced with an inconvenient situation . . . ' He brooded, the smile fading. Then he said suddenly: 'I suppose that Madame D'Aplis reached the fort?'

'She did,' Monclaire said, without looking at him.

'I thought it possible that she might, and that was why I made preparations here. Is she — er — in good health?'

Monclaire did not answer. Pavani moved

over to him. He gripped Monclaire's tunic. 'I asked you a question, *capitaine*!'

'*Je sais*. But I see no reason to reply. She did not receive much chivalry at your hands, Pavani. And neither did the others who were massacred at Tutana.'

Pavani released his grip. He said: 'You had better tell me. I do not want to have to kill you now.'

'She arrived exhausted, bruised and suffering from thirst,' Monclaire said. 'But she was recovering when I left the fort.'

'And she will remain in the fort?'

'For several days, probably.'

Pavani sank his grotesque head on his chin. He again regarded the sorrowing and excited Arabs. Then he said in an undertone which Monclaire clearly heard: 'I fear that the whole village will have to die . . . the whole village . . . I cannot leave an Arab alive . . . '

Pete, because he was next to Monclaire, also heard. So did Rex. A gasp of incredulous horror escaped fron each of them. They gazed at Pavani blankly, not yet fully believing his words. Monclaire said: 'You mean . . . you mean you are intending to slay them! Those whom you deceived into helping to attack us!'

'*Mais oui*. That is precisely so.'

'But why? You must be mad. Is this slaughter for the love of slaughter? Have you not seen enough of it, Pavani? You have murdered the officers and NCOs of your battalion. You have murdered all but one of the civilians of Tutana. You have murdered many Arabs. But to exterminate an entire village! Such a thing would be a final crime against humanity . . . '

Pavani stretched out a hand. He unfastened the flap of one of Monclaire's tunic pockets and groped within. Monclaire remained still. Pavani did not find what he wanted there, so he explored another pocket. And he drew out the captain's silver cigarette case and lighter. He lit a cigarette, then carefully put them both inside his own tunic. He blew a thin spiral of smoke into Monclaire's face.

'It is not a question of madness, *capitaine*. It is very much a matter of sanity. You must have been told why I have attacked the villages? But of course you have. The woman . . . my woman . . . will have told you. I want to create such a surge of Arab hate against the legion that it will be possible for us Zephyrs to reach the coast without interference. I intend that every garrison in Morocco and Algeria be pinned down while we are making the march. And I think you will agree that outrages against even a few villages are quite enough to start a wave of hate. News here travels very fast. And a lurid story becomes even more lurid in the retelling.'

Monclaire swallowed. He said: 'I know all that. But why slaughter these people? They have helped you — although they did not know what they were doing.'

'You are not very quick, *capitaine*. Can you not see that it is *because* they have helped me that they must die?'

Monclaire caught a faint glimmer of the ghastly truth. 'Go on,' Monclaire said softly.

'If I am to create the material for an insurrection — or a series of insurrections — the Arabs must have no doubt whatever that the legion is responsible for the outrages against their race. Now do you understand?'

'I think I do. But please explain further.'

'Certainly, *capitaine*. Now will you please consider what would happen if we were to move out of this village leaving it exactly as it is at the moment. I will tell you what would happen. The Arabs here would tell others of how one group of legionnaires came to Hagal *and helped to defend it*.' He put a hissing emphasis on the last words. Then he continued: 'Thus it would soon become obvious to the Arabs that the outrages were not the work of the legion as a whole, but only of a mutinous minority. In fact, far from rising against the legion, when the story spread the Arabs would probably turn to the legion for protection. And then, if I were to allow it, my entire plan would disintegrate . . . Now, *capitaine*, you will see why I cannot leave a single Arab alive in Hagal!'

The silence that followed was self-contained, as if the group of Zephyrs and the captives were living in a vacuum. Around them, the people of Hagal went on attending to their dead, and some were wailing. Others were still yammering threats and brandishing their assorted weapons. It was an island of silence within a sea of sound.

Pavani crossed over to his Zephyrs and spoke to them in undertones. None of the legionnaires could hear his words, but they caused blatant and bovine amusement on brutalised faces.

The Zephyrs moved away. They broke into groups of five or six, taking up positions outside the village until it became clear that they were surrounding it. Then Pavani called to an old Arab. Pavani's Arabic was fluent. He spoke easily and convincingly to the old man, who was probably the headman of Hagal.

'I wish to speak to you all,' Pavani told him. 'I have a message of great importance. I want every one of your people — each man, woman and child — to come here at once. You understand? No one must stay away.'

He was smiling as he spoke . . . smiling. And the ancient Arab was nodding vigorous agreement.

Pete thought: 'I can't let it happen. I've

117

got to warn him . . . '

Monclaire thought: 'I can't let it happen . . . '

Rex thought: 'I can't let it happen . . . '

And all of them shouted together. It was a frenzied, incomprehensible sound that erupted from their throats. Some tried to call in Arabic. Others used French — which the Arab did not understand. The result was that not a single word was clear.

The Arabs looked startled and backed away, as though fearing these wild men. But Pavani understood their motive. He did not give them the opportunity to try again. He signalled to the nearest group of Zephyrs. They ran towards the legionnaires and seized them. Lebel butts drove into their bellies, knocking them down into a helpless, sprawling mass. Then they were pulled upright and driven by blows and kicks to a point outside the village where they could no longer be heard by the doomed Arabs.

They could no longer be heard. But they could see. And they saw the unholy event as men see horrors in a nightmare.

118

They saw the villagers assembling. The bereaved were still weeping. The curious were chattering. The children clung round their parents and were wondering.

They saw the circle of Zephyrs close in on the crowd of more than two hundred Arabs. They saw the sudden puzzlement, then the panic on the brown faces. They saw the Lebels raised. They heard the crash of the satanic volley, which was repeated again and yet again.

And they saw, as the cordite smoke drifted away, that there was no longer a village of Hagal. There were only the empty hovels — and that mound of twisted bodies and limbs, which were so still it seemed impossible that they had ever lived.

★　★　★

Night was falling when, roped together, they started for Tutana. They were driven by more kicks and more oaths from the Zephyrs.

And patches of dark cloud shrouded the stars, as if the heavens themselves were mourning the horror of Hagal.

6

Commanding Officer

Lieutenant Gina blinked out of the mess-room window. He noted the patches of dark cloud in the early night sky. It looked as if a storm was coming. Then the sand would lash like pellets against the fort walls and even the sentries would have to be withdrawn from the ramparts.

Gina decided that he liked sandstorms. They gave a pleasant feeling of violence without danger. Provided, of course, one was in a safe place like Fort Valeau. He remembered Monclaire's column. They were out there in the desert looking for those damned mutineers. They would have no cover. They would have to crouch down with their backs to the wind and their blankets over their heads ... He felt a momentary sympathy for the column, but it passed when he considered the delights of the evening that lay before him.

He had asked Rene D'Aplis to be his guest at dinner. And she, having almost recovered, had accepted. It was going to be a most enjoyable *tête-à-tête* — for he had persuaded the only other member of the mess, the medical officer, to take his dinner in his bunk. Thus he, Gina, would be alone with the lady.

He would be most correct in his attitude to her, of course, just as Monclaire had ordered. He had to remember that not the least of her sufferings was the fact that she had recently lost her husband. But Gina had an idea that the charm of his own company might well open new horizons for the lady. For Professor Karlo, in that extraordinary book of his on 'How to be a Leader of Men', had generously thrown in a chapter on the conquest of women. Gina had just finished studying that section. He recalled extracts from it.

'*All women deplore indecision and admire the man who thinks quickly. Never hesitate in front of them . . . Speak from the stomach, giving resonance and tone to your voice . . . Be courteous and amusing, but be firm . . .*'

121

Gina repeated the words to himself and they gave him a glow of pure well-being. Thanks to Professor Karlo, he was armed for victory, and victory would surely be his. He hummed a merry tune as he turned from the window to inspect the dining table. It had been set with greater elegance than usual. The ebony-handled cutlery and the thin china plates were out. So was a bottle of Alsatian wine.

He would sit at the top of the table, where Monclaire normally sat. And a place for the lady had been prepared at the corner near his elbow. Nothing could go wrong. It was all going to be utterly magnificent . . .

* * *

Rene D'Aplis sipped the bitter, chicory-laden coffee. She looked tired and tense. She looked bored, too. Gina was forced to admit that, so far, the evening had not come up to expectations. He blamed the mess orderly; the fellow seemed to go about with a permanent half-smile on his stupid face. The smile had been there from the moment he had served the soup and it had been in evidence through each succeeding course. It was a cynical smile. It was a superior smile. It was the smile of a man who knows much and cannot be deceived.

Once, when serving the canned fish, Gina could have sworn that the wretch winked at him *Oui*, winked! It had not been a full, a complete wink. Merely a twitching of one eyelid. But it had been significant enough. And the insolence of it! He would have taken disciplinary action, but what disciplinary action could he take? The legionnaire might claim that it was a muscular spasm, or even deny it completely. In which case Gina had an idea that he would look rather ridiculous debating on whether the fellow had, or had not, winked at him. That, Gina told himself darkly, was the trouble with the other ranks. They could do so much to annoy an officer without risk of punishment. Yet he knew that none of them ever attempted anything of the sort with Monclaire. He envied Monclaire.

Then Gina turned again to the heavy

task of trying to make light conversation with his guest. He was feeling a little easier now, for the orderly had gone. He decided to say something that would elevate him in her eyes. Something casually modest, which would show her just what sort of man this Lieutenant Gina was. He drew in a deep breath and spoke from his stomach.

'Monclaire and I are old comrades,' he said. 'We have faced many emergencies together over the years.'

A mistake! Damn it! He should not have thrown in that bit about 'over the years' . . . his age was twenty and two months, and he had been in the legion only fourteen months.

'Really, Lieutenant? How interesting. How many years have you served with the captain?'

'Well — er — I can't remember exactly . . . so much has happened that one loses count . . . '

'I'm sure one does, Lieutenant.'

Her French had an American intonation and she pronounced the word 'lieutenant' in a ridiculous way. Gina was not so sure whether he liked the woman. And was there a hint of sudden amusement in those brown eyes of hers? Could it be that she was secretly laughing at him? Gina felt the blood rush to his face. She could not be much older than he. But she spoke to him in an almost maternal fashion, as if he were a small boy. It was most exasperating. Humiliating. Desperately, he groped for some verbal material that would indicate maturity and restore his status. 'Of course, I'm now the commanding officer here . . . I'm in complete command until Monclaire returns.'

'I know, lieutenant. The captain told me. He said he had great hopes of your becoming a really useful officer.'

Gina spluttered into his coffee. The liquid burned his hot cheeks. Monclaire had said that about him! And she had the nerve to repeat it! He loathed this woman! Monclaire was right — she was bad for morale in the fort. It would be a good thing when she was gone. He did not know what he had ever seen in her.

But she was speaking again. And the conversation had taken a surprising turn.

'Tell me,' she said. 'That soldier who came out from the fort to save me . . . he is English . . . what's his name?'

Gina dabbed his face. 'You mean Legionnaire Havers?'

'I suppose I do. You know — I don't recall much about him, except that he was very nice-looking. And he was brave and kind. Do you think I could have the opportunity to thank him?'

Gina now felt extremely annoyed. As well as being humiliated himself, it seemed that he had to listen to the woman praising one of the legionnaires! 'That will not be possible for a few days. He is with Monclaire's column.'

'Oh, I'm sorry.'

She sounded sorry, too. Gina looked at her curiously. Despite her strained nerves; despite the torn dress — which she had somehow contrived to repair; despite the entire absence of make-up and other artifices, she was very, very attractive. There could be no denying that. It was absurd that she should be showing such interest in an ordinary legionnaire, he thought.

No, Lieutenant Gina's *tête-à-tête* was not going according to plan.

★   ★   ★

Sergeaut Zatov was inspecting the sentries. He did so with the restrained hostility of an affronted apostle. He was still simmering under the injustice of being left behind in the fort while Monclaire hunted for the mutineers.

First he visited the guardroom. He glared round the confined space and was disappointed to find nothing wrong. The place was clean — not a speck of dust on the stone floor. The corporal's report form was in order. The off-duty men were resting in full kit, which was just as it should be.

Zatov mumbled through his red beard. Then he marched heavily to the rampart steps. The crash of his ascending boots was like the beating of a bass drum. He strode along the high ledge, pausing to examine each sentry. It was a thorough examination, and in each case it took the same form. He stopped a few feet away from the unhappy legionnaire and fixed a pair of smouldering eyes upon his face. If the legionnaire continued to stare into the desert night, all would probably be well. But if the man turned his head to glance back at Zatov, then all the trumpets of hell were heard. When the deprecations and imprecations had died away, Zatov would remind the wretched fellow that it was an offence to let his attention wander.

When at last the rounds were completed, Zatov leaned against the parapet near the main gates. He brooded on the injustices which man inflicted on man, with special reference to the fact that he was not at this moment with Monclaire. Then he remembered the bottle of brandy, which was carefully secreted in his bunk. His course of action was obvious: he would get drunk. Magnificently drunk, in the way that only the sons of Mother Russia understood. And each separate drink would be a toast. He would toast the late czar, in whose army he had been a pink-cheeked cadet. He would toast the whole former royal family.

He turned to go. And it was then that a bullet sliced his cap in half.

For a moment, Zatov did not fully understand what had happened. He knew only that something hot had torn at his hair and that his kepi was hanging over each ear. Then he heard the faint report from a gun. The sound was delayed because sound travels slowly. And this was a long-range shot.

Zatov took off the sliced cap and threw it away. Slowly, meticulously, he felt at his scalp. It felt as if part of it had been shaved. But there was no blood. The skin had not even been scratched. He offered a silent and informal prayer of thanks. If he had not turned away at that moment . . .

Then he glared out into the darkness. The clouds almost entirely obscured the starlight. The wind was gathering strength. He felt gusts of it blowing sand in his face. He could see nothing. Nothing at all. Not for a full half minute.

Then, to his left, he saw a distant flash and heard another report. A bullet whined high over the ramparts. A third flash and a third report confirmed his suspicions. This bullet hit the fort wall.

Zatov hurried down the steps. The

corporal of the guard was parading his men. He looked surprised when Zatov said: 'Don't sound the alarm bell.'

Then Zatov strode briskly towards the officers' mess. He was licking his lips and part of his beard as well. There was a light of anticipation in his eyes. 'This,' he announced to himself, 'is where I deal with my military chick. This is where I ask Lieutenant Gina for orders.'

★   ★   ★

For once, Gina was glad to see Sergeant Zatov. His appearance promised welcome relief from the task of trying to entertain Rene D'Aplis. But Gina was to be disappointed. Zatov did not salute because he no longer possessed a kepi, but he stood correctly at attention at the side of the mess table. He did not speak. Gina stared up at the mammoth figure, then said uncertainly: '*Oui* — you wish to speak to me, Sergeant Zatov?'

'*Non, mon officier.*'

'*Non!* You do not wish to . . . ' He felt the woman's eyes on him. And here was

Zatov trying to debase him again. It was infernally embarrassing. He continued with an attempt at firmness: ' . . . Then why are you here?'

'I await orders, *mon officier.*'

Gina groped frantically in his mind for an explanation. He found none. 'Orders! But the orders of the day were posted up last night.'

'I am sorry, *mon officier.* I thought you would wish to add to them since the fort is being attacked.'

'*Attacked!*'

'Attacked, *mon officier.*'

Gina sprang out of his chair as though impelled by a spring. 'Are you joking, Zatov? I have heard nothing. And there has been no alarm.'

Zatov was well aware that the sound of the distant shots would not carry into the secluded mess. He also knew that Gina could in no way be blamed for his ignorance. But he was not to be deterred by such trivialities. An opportunity like this did not occur every day.

'I am not joking, *officier.* Several shots have been fired at the fort. One of them damaged my cap.'

'Shots! I did not hear them.'

'They were quite loud,' Zatov lied. 'Perhaps *mon officier* was too busy . . . '

His wicked old eyes switched for a moment towards Rene D'Aplis. Gina noticed. He felt his lower lip trembling and his hands shaking. 'Sergeant Zatov! Please tell me exactly what has happened.'

There was a distinct pleading note in Gina's voice. Zatov relented. He had had his sport. The sport, which, by ancient tradition, any veteran soldier is entitled to have with a smooth-faced subaltern. He said: 'We have nothing to worry about for the moment, *mon officier*. Arabs are gathering outside the walls, but there are not many of them yet. And their shooting won't do us any harm. It is at long range and they will not be able to see much. It was a very lucky shot which cost me my cap. I don't think it will be repeated tonight.'

For the first time, Gina noticed the shaven furrow in Zatov's hair. 'How do you know there are not many Arabs? And what makes you think there is no immediate danger?'

'The gun flashes gave a good light, *officier*. There is a ring of them, but they are very widely spaced. They are shooting at the moment because they think it has a nuisance value. But they will give that up soon — when the storm breaks they will have other things to think about.'

Gina relaxed a little. Then he said plaintively: 'I suppose this is the result of the Zephyrs' attacks on the village?'

'I can think of no other reason, *officier*.'

Gina hesitated. He did not want to ask for more information and advice; the process was degrading to his rank. But he was mournfully aware of the fact that he dare not move without first consulting Zatov. He simply did not possess the requisite knowledge and experience. He had an idea that this was a situation that Professor Kerlo had not envisaged . . .

He said: 'Er — Sergeant Zatov . . . I am wondering . . . do you think I ought to give a general alarm?'

Beneath all his roguery, Zatov had a streak of kindness. It emerged now as he saw the humble and desperate look in the lieutenant's eyes. 'I see that you do not want to do so, *mon officier*. I think you are wise. It would be quite unnecessary. We are already greatly below strength, and it would be bad to exhaust the garrison by keeping a useless watch. Until the storm is over, we are safe.' As if to supplement his words, there was a sudden and powerful gust of wind. They heard the patter of driven sand against the walls.

They looked towards the window — all three of them. Rene put a hand to her throat. She shivered. Gina asked: 'How long do you think the storm will last?'

'Until daylight,' Zatov said. He turned and strode to the door. Then he paused, his fingers on the handle. He added: 'When daylight comes, I fear that many more Arabs will gather outside the fort.'

'And what then, Zatov?'

'Then I think we will be attacked.'

7

In the Wild Night

Pavani was reluctant to call a halt, but he was compelled to do so. The storm, which had given many nagging warnings of its approach, had now arrived. Wind from the great peaks of the Atlas Mountains was gathering ten thousand square miles of sand and rock in its turbulent bosom. Nothing composed of fragile flesh and blood could progress against such a tumult. The most that could be hoped for was survival.

The party of some forty men formed two circles, one within the other. The Zephyrs were on the outside, their backs to the storm and their blankets over their heads. But the legionnaires were more open to the cruel elements. They too, had blankets; but because their hands were secured and they were roped together, they could not remove them from their valises. So they sat huddled together. The sand drove through their tunics. It grazed against their skins like a trickle from a steel saw. And the cold and searching wind seemed to freeze the blood within them. There was nothing to do but to wait and endure. To endure and wait. Nothing other than to become unthinking hunks of humanity, or hibernating animals. But all of that group of prisoners retained within them the spark of resistance to overpowering force, and the desire to turn the power of nature to their own advantage.

All except one.

It was Pete who first saw the possibilities that the storm presented. The plan occurred to him when he glimpsed a solitary figure through the swirling sand that sat well inside the outer circle of men, and was nearer to the legionnaires than to the Zephyrs. His head and shoulders were covered by his blanket. But there could be no mistaking that dwarf-like form. It was Pavani.

If Pavani could be killed . . . If all of them, roped together though they were, could take advantage of the storm to creep nearer to him, then a final, simultaneous rush . . .

True, when the Zephyrs realised what had happened, they would almost certainly slay their prisoners. But there was a chance that they might not. And in any case, the prize was worth the risk. Without Pavani, without that massive and fanatical brain, the Zephyrs would become no more than a leaderless mob.

Pete did not know it, but he was reasoning in the same way that Monclaire had done several days before. Because he was secured next to Monclaire, Pete had no difficulty in crawling close to the officer. With his mouth almost pressing against Monclaire's ear, he tried to bawl a few key words. But sand drove into his throat and the message was snatched away by the screaming of the wind. Monclaire, his eyes closed to mere slits, shook his head.

Pete knew he would have to wait for a lull. It was bad, that waiting. He was suffering more than the others. The flies had made a hot hell of his open shoulder wound, and now the sand was caking onto it. It showed no sign of becoming septic, but the ugly area burned as if it had been sprayed with acid.

At last there was a brief moment when the storm abated, as though temporarily exhausted by its own fury. Pete used that moment to try again. He shouted the word 'Pavani.' He followed it with three others, each precisely articulated. 'Try to kill . . . '

Then the short lull ended. But Monclaire had heard and he understood. He turned his head and peered through his nearly closed lids. He kept blinking to clear them. But he discerned that small huddled figure. And the muscles of Monclaire's wan, dust-caked face twisted into a parody of a smile. He nodded. But no action could be taken yet. Every legionnaire must understand before they could move. With the rope joining them together, they were like the separate limbs of a single body. They had to act in concert, or not at all.

And so — more waiting. Waiting and praying that there would be another lull

in the storm; another brevity of comparative quiet when the message could be
passed round. Ten minutes passed. Or
perhaps it was half an hour. There was no
means of gauging time in that screeching
tempest. But it came — another temporary calm.

Pete got the words out to Rex. The
American did not pause to acknowledge
them. He twisted round and repeated
them to the next man. Monclaire spoke to
Corporal Offlan. The corporal was close
to Monclaire, now they had formed a
small circle. Offlan hesitated before he
repeated the message, but Monclaire did
not notice. He only saw the ring of
nodding heads, like dim ghosts in the
wild night. And each of them was trying
to focus his eyes on Pavani. The order had
got round. All understood what was
planned.

The sandstorm was now at its peak.
There were times when visibility was
absolutely nil and the act of breathing
became a frantic agony.

This was the time.

If they could force their minds and

sinews to take them over those few yards which divided them from Pavani.

If they could reach Pavani before another of those lulls made it possible for the Zephyrs to see them

If, acting together, they could kill him before help came to him.

If . . .

That eternal conjunction was never more important than now.

Monclaire made the first move. Slowly, he twisted to his knees. Pete followed — and he felt stabs of pain in his stiff limbs. The wind slammed at his back, threatening to push him onto his face. He sobbed under the buffeting and a sudden increase of pain from his wound.

One by one, the others got to their knees, too. Corporal Offlan was the last to do so. If the others had bothered to look they would have seen a strangely wild expression on the thin face of the newly promoted NCO.

Monclaire tried to stand. He swayed and stumbled but he was almost in an upright position when he suddenly pitched on to his back. Pete knew the reason. A pulling at his wrists told him that it was the rope that joined them that had pulled Monclaire down. In their mutual shuffling, the two had moved too far away from each other. They moved closer, so as to allow more slack in the connecting line. Then Monclaire tried again. This time there was no mishap, but he found obvious difficulty in keeping his feet. So did Pete. Then Pete saw the tall, lean form of Rex rise at his side, and he made out the ascending silhouettes of the others. Presently all were standing — all except Offlan. The corporal made two laborious attempts, falling back to his knees each time. After the second attempt he remained kneeling. The man next to Offlan twitched at the rope, but Corporal Offlan did not move; he remained as though at prayer. Pete saw Monclaire's lips moving; he was enunciating an oath. By instinct, they all knew that Offlan could stand if he wanted to. He did not want to. Why? Because he was afraid. Offlan did not want to see Pavani murdered. That much became grimly obvious as they blinked at him through the swirling sand. Offlan had seen what the Zephyrs could do. He feared the consequences of slaying their leader.

Corporal Offlan was not really to blame. He was a good lecture room soldier. He was a good barrack square soldier. In both those places he could absorb instruction easily and impart it efficiently. In action, he could be ordinarily brave. But he could not be brave for very long. He had little staying power, little fibre. Offlan's main misfortune was that he made his best impression on the wrong people; he fawned upon officers. Inevitably, some officers liked being fawned upon. They were not the best type. But they recommended Offlan to the corporals' school. At the school, his diligence and anxiety to please made a big impression on the instructors. So they posted him to Monclaire's unit with a suggestion that he would make a good NCO. And, by tradition, Monclaire had been bound to adopt the suggestion. But those instructors, their minds cluttered by theory, had not been able to detect the lack of essential toughness in Offlan. And Monclaire had not had the opportunity to detect it — until now.

Monclaire cursed himself for his decision to bring Offlan with him. If only Zatov had been there. Zatov had wanted to come.

Instinctively, they gathered round the kneeling Offlan. They prodded him with their boots. He did not move. They hauled him upright, but immediately after they released him he slumped to the sand again.

His nerve had gone. He was a hollow shell of a man. But he was making it impossible for them to move. Offlan was an anchor that fastened them to that spot. If only they could break the rope which tied him to them ... But that was impossible, since their hands were lashed behind them.

There was only one possible course. They must drag him along, between them. Monclaire gave the signal and they started. Normally it would have been an easy task, for Offlan was no great weight. But the storm made it almost unendurable. Sometimes one man falling would drag all the others down. And Offlan was like a corpse. He lay on his back, allowing himself to be pulled inch by inch. He neither had the grace to stand up nor the spirit to resist.

And the moment came when they could pull him no further. At first, they thought it was because their strength had gone. But there was another reason: Offlan's shoulders had caught against a large imbedded rock. It must have been uncovered by the storm, for its edges had not been smoothed by exposure. They were sharp. And the rope had passed over one of those edges.

It seemed as if they all saw the possibility at once, for they stumbled towards the spot simultaneously. But Rex got there first. It was probably fortunate that he did so, for he was the strongest of the group. He lay on his back over the rock and groped with his bound hands for the rope. He was able to grip it with the ends of his fingers. Then, in that tortuous position, he started to rub the hemp against the sharp rock. It was agonizing work. The sand on his sweating face caked like wet powder. He had a paroxysm of coughing as the stuff caught in his throat. Several times his fingers slipped and on each occasion the rock gashed them. But, after a seeming eternity, the rope parted. And Rex was staggering to his feet. His hands were a scarlet mess.

But they were free of Corporal Offlan now. The human anchor had been cast away . . . And Offlan himself was getting onto one knee. He waved at them wildly. There was fear and confusion in that gesture, but they did not notice it. Offlan no longer mattered. He was no longer one of them.

Again they turned towards where Pavani was huddled — eight reeling, dazed men on a mission of murder. That they only caught infrequent glimpses of Pavani did not matter. In fact, it was an advantage, for it meant that their own chances of being seen were correspondingly less. Monclaire led them through a semi-circle, so that they would approach the Italian from the rear.

During the last few yards the storm reached a new fury. They had to throw themselves flat, for there was a danger of being carried by the wind past Pavani. And if once they got in front of him, he could scarcely fail to see them.

They had to remain prone for minutes. Then the wind abated slightly. Wearily, they rose again to their feet and shuffled on. Pavani was near now. Very near. Each of them knew that when they saw him again he would be within striking dustance. Then . . . then they would gather round him . . . they would kill him . . . It would not be brutal. Nothing could be brutal which killed Pavani.

The clouds of sand cleared. They saw him. He was no more than a couple of paces away and directly ahead.

But he was standing upright. He was facing them. A pistol was in his hand. And Corporal Offlan was cowering at Pavani's side.

★ ★ ★

It was morning and the storm had gone. Only the jagged immensity of the newly created dunes hinted of the fury that was no more. The legionnaires, their legs

146

bound now, lay on the rapidly warming sand. Pavani stood in front of them.

Watching him, they were puzzled. The man was crazy, yet he did not run to type. He could appear to be a model of sanity. That was how he appeared now, for there was an air of affronted good taste about him. He regarded them carefully, almost sympathetically. Then he spoke to Monclaire.

'I congratulate you, *capitaine*. You are a courageous man, and so are the men who serve you.'

Monclaire did not answer. He did not feel courageous that moment. He was aware of only one fact — that he was exhausted. Physically and mentally, he was done. Useless. He was the withered core of the fruit; he was ash from the flame. He represented all things that had had their day and were spent beyond recall. But he was not alone in that. To varying degrees, the others felt much the same. And there was a common surprise that Pavani had not killed them that night. Each felt a remote form of curiosity about the delay.

Pavani produced Monclaire's cigarette

case. He lit a cigarette from it with Monclaire's lighter. Then he added: 'It seems to me, *capitaine*, rather a pity that such devotion, such loyalty, should be accorded to a wrong cause such as yours.'

Monclaire heard the words vaguely. He found himself repeating them. Then the full incredible meaning occurred to him. Pavani was preaching on human values! He did not intend answering. Yet Monclaire said, faintly: 'Go on — you interest me.'

'I thought I would. You see, *capitaine*, when your corporal warned me of what you intended to do during the storm, I did two things. First, as you know, I took steps to protect myself. Then, I gave the matter much thought — I think a lot, *capitaine*.

'I asked myself a question. I said to myself, 'Pavani, would not men such as these legionnaires be a great help to you during your march to the coast? Most of them, at least, are intelligent. Such intelligence would be of great value since, at the moment, you command only fools.'

'That is what I said to myself,

capitaine. It is reasonable, is it not? You must be able to see that, even with the legion pinned down by Arab insurgents, the long march will present many difficulties. These difficulties would be much less forbidding if you and your men were with us . . . but it is you in particular that I want. Your experience of desert marching would be invaluable.'

The fatigue was leaving Monclaire. It was leaving the others, too. After a long silence, Monclaire said: 'You have done very well so far, Pavani. What is it that you fear?'

Pavani wagged his ungainly head. 'Fear! I fear nothing. But I would be a fool if I did not take every possible measure to make my task easier.'

'You say you want me in particular on the march.'

'That is so. The others — yes, if they wish. But I will be frank, *capitaine*. It is you, with your experience and initiative, who intrigue me.'

Monclaire's brain was racing. It was collating the probabilities and possibilities. And it arrived at a certain significant conclusion. He said: 'Would it be that you are afraid of getting lost on such a march, Pavani?'

He showed no annoyance. He smiled and nodded pleasantly. 'I thought you would deduce as much. You are right, *capitaine*. Except that I do not actually fear getting lost — it is only the possibility of delay.' Pavani inhaled deeply. There was something gross about the way he smoked, as if he was satisfying a carnal lust. He continued: 'It needs great experience to find one's way with certainty over these trackless wastes. But do not mistake me. I alone could get the Zephyrs to the coast. But I think that you could get us there much more quickly.'

'*Oui* . . . perhaps I could. And your terms?'

'Terms? They are obvious enough, *capitaine*. In return for your services your lives will be spared.'

'*Dieu*! You speak to me as if I were an imbecile! Do you expect me to place any trust in your word?'

'I do, *capitaine*, for you have so little choice in the matter. If you refuse my offer, you will all die as soon as we reach Tutana. You have seen enough to know that I do not joke about such things.'

Monclaire seemed to consider. Then he said: 'This proposal of yours . . . it is not new, is it? You say it occurred to you after we tried to kill you. But I do not believe that. I think it has been in your mind ever since we were captured at Hagal. But you have decided to put it to us now because our spirits are obviously low and we look as if we will agree to anything. I am right, am I not?'

Pavani laughed gently, sibilantly. 'You are perceptive, *capitaine*! And you are so right. You have realized, of course, that if I had not had work in mind for you, I would never have bothered to take you alive. But come . . . you know my terms. It is not a difficult decision for you to make. Do you accept — and live? Or do you refuse — and die?'

Monclaire looked at the trussed men who sat round him. There was an utter lack of expression on their faces. They avoided his eye. All of them stared blankly into the middle distance — even the

Englishman, even the American. There was no exception. And Monclaire sighed. He knew that this decision was his, and his alone. The handful of men around him could give him no help. Because they were mortals, they wanted to live. Because they were men — real men — they had a strong basic honour that transcended all their outward crudities. They did not want to betray it.

Was the issue worth dying for? For the second time within twenty-four hours, Monclaire had to face this question. He had little doubt that Pavani was speaking the truth when he claimed that he could guide his Zephyrs to the coast unaided. The Italian simply wished to enlist greater experience than his own to ensure that the march was completed as quickly as possible. But even if they refused and died, the march should be completed. It would probably take days, or even weeks, longer than necessary. But Pavani would get them there.

Monclaire felt that if he had been alone, he would have refused. He had seen death too often and in too many forms to be unduly afraid of it. But he was not alone. His answer would decide whether the others lived or died — for the time being, at least.

'I accept,' he said. 'I will guide you to the coast on the condition that our lives are spared.'

There was a peculiar shuffling movement among the legionnaires. All of a sudden, their breathing became quick and very audible. Monclaire glanced at them. They were relieved, yet they were uneasy. They were glad of his decision, yet they were ashamed of it. It was all clear on their grimed and unshaven faces; on every face except one. Legionnaire Pete Havers offered a contrast to the rest. There was a half smile on his lips and he was nodding approval. The Englishman, it seemed, saw possibilities in the situation; possibilities that were also forming in Monclaire's own mind.

Then they again heard Pavani's voice. It destroyed that faint hope even before it was fully formed. 'I must warn you,' Pavani said, 'it may be that you have some notion of misleading us on the desert march. Guiding us to nowhere, perhaps, so we will die of thirst and exposure. Or taking us into a legion base. If you have any such puerile plans, you must forget them. I am not an expert on direction-finding, but I can take a simple compass bearing. I will know if we are going the proper way.'

He dropped his smoked cigarette into the sand, inserted a hand under an ill-fitting officer's tunic and scratched his hair-matted chest. There was that distant, thoughtful look about him. Then he turned to his Zephyrs, who were sprawling some yards off. 'The corporal,' Pavani called. 'Corporal Offlan — bring him here!'

The legionnaires shuffled again, staring towards the Zephyrs. They had almost forgotten about Offlan. He was not important. Even in the moment when they had realized that he had betrayed them, he had not seemed important. Offlan was, it seemed, one of nature's little men, and even his infamies could not make him appear big.

But they were surprised when he

emerged from the midst of the Zephyrs, where he had apparently been sitting. He walked with a strut. There was an ingratiating smile on his lean face as he approached Pavani. Somehow, he had even managed to remove the worst ravages of the storm from his uniform. The buttons twinkled in the morning sun and there was scarcely a rumple in the tunic.

When he was three paces from Pavani, he came to a brisk halt. His right hand flashed up in a parade-ground salute. Monclaire, Pete, Rex — all of them — watched incredulously, but with dawning comprehension. Offlan was the type of person who could not live without having a boot to lick. Until recently, he had been happy carrying out this unwanted service to Monclaire. And now, it had to be Pavani. To Offlan's mind it was a perfectly logical metamorphosis. He worshipped at the shrine of power. Power was no longer represented by Monclaire; it was embodied in the form of Pavani. Therefore, Pavani would receive all Offlan's dubious loyalty.

It occurred to Pete that there were

many other Offlans in the world, and not all of them were soldiers. In the more sedate walks of life they were the people who automatically supported the loudest voice in an argument; the people who found it natural to side with the mob if the mob looked like having its own way. One of their guiding principles was that they would never be in a minority.

Pavani observed the salute critically. He nodded approval. Then he said: 'Corporal — Monclaire and his men are going to co-operate with me from now on. I am very pleased.'

'And I am very pleased,' Offlan echoed.

Listening, Monclaire gave a snort. '*Mon Dieu*,' he muttered. 'At least I am relieved of one burden!' Some of them managed to laugh — as men will always seize an opportunity for laughter amid tragedy.

Offlan remained rigidly at attention while Pavani said: 'It therefore seems that our march to the coast will be much easier.'

'Yes, indeed. It will be much easier.'

'And you, Corporal Offlan, have earned my gratitude for saving my life.'

'I am glad to have earned your gratitude for saving your life.'

'But, corporal, you will not receive it!'

'I will not — not receive it?'

'Exactly. You will not receive the gratitude that you have so richly earned. But that is one of the injustices of life. Instead of rewarding you suitably, I am going to kill you — or, more correctly, I am going to cause you to be killed.'

Offlan's stance became less rigid. He raised one protesting hand. The movement was jerky and artificial, like that of a doll. 'You are going to cause me to be killed? But I do not understand!'

'I thought you wouldn't. I will try to explain. You are a traitor, are you not?'

Offlan tried to answer, but no sound came forth. Only a quivering bulge in his throat showed that he was attempting to articulate.

'I see that you agree,' Pavani added smoothly.

At last Offlan got the words out. 'But I'm not a traitor . . . no! I saved your life! You've said so yourself! How can I be a traitor? I am loyal — loyal to you! I would do anything for you . . . anything . . . you are making a mistake . . . you can't kill me!'

Pavani yawned. Then he said: 'Yesterday you were loyal to Captain Monclaire, were you not?'

'Yes — I mean no — I . . . '

'Precisely, corporal. Your loyalty is a flimsy thing, and I have no use for it. Neither, I imagine, have the legionnaires whom you betrayed. Therefore, I think it just that Captain Monclaire should have the opportunity of — er — of executing you.'

Monclaire started. He twisted in his bonds, as if trying to stand upright. 'I . . . you think that I will kill Offlan? *Mais non*!'

Pavani looked genuinely puzzled. 'But why not, *capitaine*? He has betrayed you, his officer.'

'That is a matter which concerns only me at the moment. In spite of the fact that I am the prisoner of a mob of mutineers, I am still bound by French military law. And Offlan is still entitled to the protection of that law. He cannot be punished by the legion until he has been tried and found guilty by a general court martial.'

'But, *capitaine*,' Pavani purred, 'are we not being rather academic? His offence is punishable by death according to military law. Isn't that correct?'

'It is.'

'Then I am giving you the opportunity of administering your laws! Come. Monclaire, I will give you back your pistol — with one bullet in the breech. Use it to kill Offian! It appeals to my sense of the bizarre. And, meanwhile in case you still have murderous ideas towards me, I will watch from a distance.'

'*Non* — I refuse.'

Pavani seemed deeply disappointed. He looked once more at the shaking Offlan. He said to him: 'I am sorry, Corporal. It seems that you are not to die at the hands of your former comrades.'

Offlan's shaking became less pronounced. There was a glimmer of hope on his taut, agonized features. 'I — I didn't think they would do it,' he bleated

Pavani said: 'It is unfortunate for you that they will not. A bullet froin Captain

Monclaire would be a much quicker way of dying than the one my Zephyrs will inflict on you.'

Offlan's flicker of optimism was gone. 'You mean you are going to ... to ... because Captain Monclaire refuses!'

'We are. And it will be a painful process, Offlan. You may have heard of it, for it is a system which was once much favoured by the Touareg Arabs.'

Monclaire had twisted himself into a crouching position. He glared at Pavani like a chained hound. '*Batard*! You cannot do that to him!'

'It will be done now, *capitaine*, since you refuse to grant Offlan the mercy of a quick death.'

Monclaire was breathing noisily, as if he had been running long and far. He said: 'Very well ... I will shoot him!'

Offlan gazed frantically at Monclaire. Then at Pavani. And then he threw himself on his face at Pavani's feet. He uttered slobbering and largely incomprehensible appeals. He wept like an hysterical woman, his tears wetting the sand. Pavani looked down at him for a while in the manner of a scholar observing an interesting problem in psychology. Then he said: 'Corporal Offlan! This is not in the best traditions of the French Foreign Legion! Please get up from that ridiculous position. This is your chance to be a hero!'

Suddenly Offlan ceased to plead; ceased to weep. He rose slowly and unsteadily. His face was blotched with tear stains and sand. His tunic had entirely lost its recent smartness. He made a slow circle on his heels, looking at the legionnaires, then the Zephyrs. Then he spoke. There was a tremble in his voice, but the words were clear. He addressed them to Pavani. 'I am not afraid any more,' he said. 'I think . . . I think fear must be like pain. When it becomes too much to bear, it passes . . . '

Pavani shrugged his shoulders. He crossed over to the Zephyrs and spoke to them. Then he walked away while Monclaire was being untied. When Monclaire's pistol was returned to him, Pavani was standing nearly three hundred yards away — well out of range.

Monclaire rubbed life into his cramped wrists. Then he said: 'Turn your back to

me, Corporal Offlan . . . it will be quick
. . . you will know nothing.'

Offlan did not answer. But he shook his
head. Monclaire did not attempt to argue.
He thrust the pistol out at arm length and
squeezed the trigger.

Probably Corporal Offlan was at peace
in those moments before he died, for he
had returned to his old master.

8

Invitation from Zatov

Sergeant Zatov's patience — never his most outstanding quality — was being heavily strained. He stood mightily upon the ramparts and boomed thunderous phrases at Lieutenant Gina. 'But look at them!' he declaimed with a broad gesture at the distant Arab cordon round the fort. 'Look, I say! There are hundreds of them out there and more are arriving every hour. Soon they will attack. And what will happen? I, Zatov, will tell you! They will force the gates. They will storm these walls. They may not do it the first time nor the second. But they will do it, *mon officier*. They will do it because fifty of our men are out in the desert with Captain Monclaire!' He scratched his beard ferociously and fixed his burning eyes on Gina.

Gina shifted uneasily from one foot to

another. 'But I don't see what we can do,' he muttered. 'And it's not my fault that the garrison has been left in this weak state. I can't help thinking that Monclaire made a mistake in leaving us.'

'A mistake! Captain Monclaire did not make a mistake! He has done the only thing possible — he is trying to deal with the trouble at its source. Even now, he may have killed or captured that *batard* Pavani. Don't you see, *mon officier*, that the captain could not possibly guess that the Arabs would rise so quickly? Those Zephyrs . . . '

Gina put a hand to his head. It was aching. And he was confused. A conversation with Zatov in his present mood was like sitting inside a bass drum. 'Yes, I see that, Zatov. But what can we do if the Arabs attack except try to fight them off?'

'*Mon officier*, we can avoid fighting!'

Before answering, Gina found time to wish that Professor Karlo had had the opportunity of dealing with Zatov. 'Avoid fighting, Sergeant? But I don't understand. Surely we can't decide a matter such as that. It is something the Arabs will decide . . . '

'No! With respect, *mon officier*, you speak like a fool! I would not think of saying that you are one. But I say that you speak like one. Why are those Arabs out there? I ask you, why?'

'Because . . . '

'Exactly so! Because they think that the legion has murdered their innocent people and despoiled their villages. Thinking that, they are right to seek vengeance. But we know the truth. We know that the outrages are not the work of the legion, but of mutinous criminals. Why should we not let the Arabs know that, too? And if we could convince them that even now a column is out and trying to find the leader of the mutiny, they would have no cause to attack us. They might even help us, for these are not truly warriors. They are ordinary people.'

Gina tried to think. He tried to forget Zatov's overpowering presence and assess the situation for himself. He wanted to make some caustic and brilliant remark that would at once crush and quiet Zatov. He racked his brains. 'Er — please go on, Zatov,' he said.

'Thank you, *mon officier*. I suggest that you allow me to go out to speak to the Arabs. Let me do it immediately, before the first blood is spilled. I, Zatov, can speak their tongue. I am skilled at explaining things. They will listen to me.'

Gina thought: 'If he speaks to them as he is speaking to me, they will certainly listen to him. They'll have no choice about it. Half of Morocco will be able to hear him.' But he had not the nerve to voice the comment. Instead, he said: 'I think they would shoot you down before you got near them, Sergeant.'

'Shoot me down?' Zatov pointed to himself in astonishment, as though Gina was doubting one of the immortals. 'Shoot me? Ah no, *mon officier*. The Arabs are a curious people. They will want to know why it is that I leave the fort alone and unarmed. And I will also take a white flag. They know what that means.'

Gina was uncomfortably aware that Zatov was talking as if his mission had already been approved. 'I'm not sure, Sergeant. I'm afraid that . . . '

'Not sure? But you are joking, *mon*

officier! I laugh! *Ha!* You are a man of wit. I, Zatov, appreciate men of wit. I am sorry there is no time for me to listen further. I must start immediately . . . '

* * *

The sun was still low in the sky when Zatov left the fort. And, being Zatov, there were no half measures about the manner in which he set about his mission. He departed with the demeanour of a wise man going forth to spread his virtue. His head was high and his red beard glowed magnificently. Each confident stride thudded heavily into the newly driven sand. In one of his enormous hands he clutched a square of white material. This was intended to be his flag of truce, but he held it as if it was a pocket handkerchief.

Yet Zatov, despite his apparent fool-hardiness, was a shrewd man. He knew the Arabs. And he knew there was little danger while the Arabs remained ignorant of his purpose in leaving the fort alone. The danger would come when he had talked to them. If he failed to convince them . . .

He made for a place, almost directly ahead of the gates, where a tent was being unloaded from the back of a camel. This, he deduced, was where the headmen must be gathering. The tent was being pitched some four hundred yards from the fort — a long walk under such circumstances, for the Arabs scurried into groups, pointing and excitedly discussing him. Some made menacing gestures with their muskets.

Zatov kept glittering eyes fixed firmly on his objective. Yet he saw much that confirmed his earlier suspicions. He saw that very few of the Arabs belonged to the traditional warrior tribes. Nearly all of them were the normally peaceful men of the villages. They held unfamiliar and aged firearms in fumbling hands. But that did not alter the fact that they would be capable of storming the lightly garrisoned fort. They gathered round Zatov as he neared the tent site, but they did not attempt to hinder him. He pushed through the sea of robes with the gentle omnipotence of a warship entering harbour.

A dozen elderly headmen were awaiting him. It was fortunate for Zatov that his self-confidence was almost completely unshakable. If it had been otherwise, he would certainly have despaired by now. For the headmen, scrawny and frail though most of them were, exuded an atmosphere of absolute hate; absolute contempt. It was reflected in the depths of their dark old eyes, in the twist of their thin brown mouths, in the tilt of their heads, and in the way they fingered the hilts of the knives.

Zatov stopped when only a few inches from them. He towered above them, as he towered above all men. He commanded attention; he demanded respect. Yet his normal arrogance was gone. Zatov was about to reveal a new aspect of his extraordinary personality. He was about to become the diplomat; the negotiator.

The headmen waited for him to speak. He took his time, carefully assembling the most telling Arabic phrases. Then he began in what was, for him, a soft pitch. But gradually the volume increased. His gestures became more and more emphatic.

None of the headmen attempted to interrupt. They listened carefully. So did the many hundreds of other Arabs who had gathered within earshot.

And when at last Zatov had finished, the headmen stared at him steadily. He stared back. They were the first to lower their eyes. They questioned him. Always, Zatov's answers were simple and convincing. Then, after an uneasy pause, one of them said: 'If you do not lie to us . . . if it is true that even now your captain may have captured or killed the evil one who slew our people, when will he return to you?'

Zatov shrugged. 'Today, tomorrow, who knows? I told you that he has gone to Hagal and he plans to wait there for them. He may have to wait for days. Or perhaps he has already killed their leader and is marching back to the fort.'

The headmen looked at each other. Then, spontaneously, they withdrew into the tent, which had now been raised, leaving Zatov outside. He heard only the indistinct mumble of their voices as they discussed his message. But the Russian was not one to waste time. He raised both hands in a signal for silence to the gabbling crowd. They became silent. And they were noticeably less hostile as Zatov repeated, so as to make doubly clear, the facts of the Zephyr mutiny.

He was finishing when the headmen emerged. One of them spoke and his cracked old voice seemed painfully feeble after the sergeant's booming tones. This headman said: 'You come to us with a strange story and we cannot yet believe that your words are true. We know only what our eyes have seen. We have seen the bodies of our people who have been struck down even as they slept. And those who lived in the villages say they were attacked by men clad as legionnaires. But you have spoken to us of a woman — a white woman — who escaped from the vandals. You say she is now within the fort. Let us see her. Let us speak to her. If we can do that, we may believe the tale you tell.'

Zatov nodded. 'You can speak to her. And you can speak to my officer, too.'

'We are not concerned with your officer — only with this woman of whom you tell. Three of us will come back with you to the fort. But remember this — if we are harmed in any way while within the walls, there will be a terrible vengeance!'

'You will see the white woman and you will not be harmed,' Zatov said.

★ ★ ★

The room, normally occupied by Monclaire, seemed vastly crowded. Gina sat uncomfortably behind the commanding officer's desk. Rene D'Aplis was in the only other chair. The three Arabs were grouped round her, questioning, questioning, questioning . . .

And, dominating it all with his presence, was Zatov. It was Zatov who helped Rene when she failed to understand some unfamiliar twist of Arabic dialect. It was Zatov who, unprompted, thought of offering the headmen wine from the officer's mess. It was Zatov who, in brief snatches, lectured his officer on the new developments. Gina felt superfluous. But he also felt glad that Sergeant Zatov had taken over. He knew that without Zatov, the fort would now be under attack.

The Arabs were in that room for nearly an hour. At the end of it, they bowed to Rene D'Aplis, who looked strained but composed. One of them, turning to Gina and Zatov, said: 'The woman, too, speaks well. But we have suffered too much to put our trust in words alone. We must see this patrol, which you say is in the desert. How long will it be before they must return?'

Gina looked at a desk calendar. The date on it was *Juin* 17. He made a simple calculation. 'They will be back in three days at the most,' he said. 'They are carrying only pack supplies and those will be exhausted by then.'

The Arab bowed acknowledgment. He said: 'Then we will wait outside this fort for three days. If in that time we see the patrol coming back with Zephyr prisoners, then we will know that you have not been false and we shall depart in peace. But . . . if, in three days, no patrol appears, then we shall assault the fort and slay every legionnaire within it. Aye . . . and we shall even slay this woman also . . . '

9

The Flames

Monclaire pulled a diary from his breast pocket. In the space allotted to *Juin* 17 he wrote —

'*Arrived Tutana two hours ago at about three p.m. Zephyrs have given us quarters in former administrative offices. We are no longer in bonds, but a heavy guard outside.*'

He sighed, reinserted the pencil in the spine of the diary, and replaced it in the pocket. It was, he reflected, pure habit that caused him to note down the events of the day. In the ordinary way, he made such notes on his pad of company report forms. But those forms, like most of his other possessions, had been taken away from him. So the little diary was a substitute. Not that there was really much point in making further entries. He was unlikely to find himself being disciplined for failing to do so. But, he told himself, habit was a hard taskmaster and one might as well obey . . .

Monclaire sighed again. Then he looked at his seven men. They lay sprawled on the bare stone floor, heads pillowed on their kepis. Around them was the wreckage of the office furniture — a token of the day the Zephyrs had rebelled. It was strange, Monclaire thought, that when men slept they looked like children. The oldness and the bitterness of the years seemed to fall away. They became again, for a few brief hours, what they had once been when their world was young.

That Polish legionnaire, whose boots were balanced precariously on his chest, had re-enlisted no less than five times. That meant twenty-five years' service. He had fought in the wars against the Riffs and the Touaregs. He had fought many other and less distinguished engagements in the drunken atmosphere of the wine shops. He had given his life to the business of soldiering. Which, in blunt terms, meant that he was a disciplined killer. But he did not look like a killer now, while he slept. He was very still. A half-smile had softened his hard face. The back of one hand was pressed against his forehead. Like a child.

The Englishman, Pete Havers, was like a boy in a restless dream. He turned uneasily. His fingers twitched. And sometimes he muttered something. It was easy to see what Legionnaire Havers had looked like twenty years ago. He had looked very English in the way of the well-bred English. His horizons had been limited by the boundaries of some famous school. His ambitions had been symbolised by an oval ball and a cricket bat . . .

The tall American, Rex Tyle, was in one way different from the others. He looked young as he slept, yet there was a perpetual youth about him at other times, too. He was like so many of his countrymen: he possessed a magnificent zest for life. He approached any and every situation at full gallop. It was immature. It was a characteristic that led to many mistakes. But it could achieve many unexpected successes, also . . .

Monclaire realised that he was as tired

as the others. Yet he had not thought of sleep for himself until his men were resting. Habit again. He yawned and looked for a place on the floor. Then through the barred window, he saw the malformed figure of Pavani. He was crossing from the place where several ugly villas were placed — villas in which the oil engineers and their families had lived. The late afternoon sun was shining directly onto the Italian's features. And Monclaire noticed with a mild shock that much of the fanaticism had faded. There was a composed expression on his face, as if the madman who had once been a poet had gone back to his verse and was finding peace again.

Monclaire saw a Zephyr sentry shuffle out of the way as Pavani entered the office building. He heard the key turn quietly in the lock. The door of their improvised prison opened. Pavani stood on the threshold and glanced round at the sleeping legionnaires. Then he smiled at Monclaire. And Monclaire now felt a strange horror. For it was an attractive smile — a smile that under ordinary circumstances, would be answered in kind. It was completely, grotesquely unfitting. It was like watching the devil put on an angel's wings.

Pavani said softly: 'I am glad to have found you awake, *capitaine*. I feared that you might be sleeping.'

'I shall be in a few minutes, I trust.'

'But of course! You must have all the rest you can get. I merely called to tell you that we are starting our march at first daylight tomorrow.'

Monclaire stroked the black bristles on his chin. He said: 'It is a long march to the coast, Pavani. It will take several weeks, even if there are no incidents. And it will be very exhausting. You are not allowing us much time to recover from our . . . our ordeals, are you?'

Pavani shrugged. He remained in the open doorway, within easy call of his Zephyrs. 'You are all hard men. Surely you will be ready after a night's rest.'

'One of us may not,' Monclaire said, and he jerked his thumb in the direction of Pete Havers. 'That man has an open wound. You refused to let us dress it. Do you remember?'

Pavani glanced at Pete. 'But it is

dressed now, *capitaine*. And it is not very serious, is it?'

'We dressed the wound ourselves, as soon as our hands were freed. It should have been done twenty-four hours earlier. You are right when you say it is not very serious, but it is very painful. We must wait a little longer because of him.'

Pavani held forth his hands in a gesture of supplication. 'It is no use, *capitaine*! You are trying to gain time. You are hoping that some miracle may occur to save you from accompanying us on the march. But there is no chance of that. None at all. Listen to me! We have a radio station here. You know that, do you not?'

'Of course I do. You used it to inform Sadazi of your mutiny. Why?'

'There was always a chance that the legion might hear of what had happened through some incident. So I had to make it clear that if there was any attack on us we would destroy the oil line. I gave the information so as to ensure our own safety. But I digress. I want you to know quite clearly, *capitaine*, that your comrades in the legion garrisons are too preoccupied just now to worry about you. We have, for example, just picked up a signal sent from your own Fort Valeau to Dini Sadazi. It said that the fort is surrounded by hostile Arabs.'

'*Mon Dieu!*' Monclaire's exclamation was involuntary.

'You are surprised?'

'I was hoping that it would not happen so soon.'

'Then you have been too optimistic. But let me tell you more. It appears that the Arabs have undertaken to go away under certain conditions.'

'Go on — go on, Pavani.'

'They are awaiting your return to the fort — with Zephyr prisoners.'

Monclaire turned away. He stared through the window, but he saw nothing of the ugly shambles that was Tutana. He saw only the fort. His fort! The place he had almost denuded so as to end up like this, a prisoner of the mutineers! And worse than that, a man who had agreed to co-operate with the mutineers! The fact that he had agreed in the hope of finding some way of thwarting Pavani did not affect the issue. Had ever a soldier man-oeuvred himself and his men into such a catastrophe? Never!

He heard Pavani's voice again. It was smooth and conciliatory. 'You would be wrong to feel too bitter, *capitaine*. And you must not blame yourself. Let me be frank with you — I thought that your tactics in coming out to seek me were imaginative and courageous. If you had been dealing with any man other than I, you would probably have achieved a spectacular success. But you did not know one thing, *capitaine*. One vital thing. You did not know that I, the leader of the mutineers, can see further than other men. How could you be expected to realise that since I have given my life to the arts of violence and intrigue, I would find no difficulty in foreseeing the movements of an orthodox soldier?'

He paused, as if expecting Monclaire to turn. But Monclaire remained staring out of the window. Pavani went on: 'So would it not be better if you accepted the situation? Could we not work together amicably, now that I have won?'

Another pause. Again Monclaire remained still. He was only vaguely aware of Pavani's words. He saw the group of Zephyrs who were rolling greasy barrels into the adjoining building. He was still thinking, thinking, thinking . . .

'We are both intelligent men, *capitaine*. The long march need not be unpleasant, for we would have much to talk about if you are reasonable. I could explain to you my beliefs. I could show you that when I am brutal it is only because of necessity and in order that out of the blood and suffering a new and completely free form of life may develop . . . You may find that there is more in the theory of social anarchy than you think, *capitaine*. More than a mere bomb hurled from a crowd. It is an idea that has intrigued the minds of many great thinkers. It could intrigue *your* mind, Monclaire, if you will let it. Now that there is no further cause for strife, may we not forget the past and look to the future . . . ?'

At last Monclaire turned.

He was smiling. But it was a humorless caricature of a smile. He said: 'I think the

English have a cliché about pouring oil on troubled waters.'

'They have, *capitaine*, but it is not apposite. There is no trouble now. All that is over. I am only trying to show you that you might as well co-operate with me in spirit as well as in fact.'

'I will think about it, Pavani. Meantime, you are determined to start the march at dawn?'

'Quite determined. The conditions are ideal. Everything I planned has come to pass, except . . . except . . . ' He hesitated, fumbling for words. Monclaire looked at him with curiosity. He actually seemed to be in the grip of an emotion he could not control.

'Go on, Pavani. Except for what?'

He answered, almost savagely. 'Except for her!'

'You mean Madame D'Aplis?'

'I do.'

'*Dieu*! You are being insular in your outlook for an anarchist! She has slipped through your fingers — but even you, Pavani, will be able to find another woman!'

'Another woman! You fool, *capitaine*! Don't you understand? She was more than just a woman to me! She was the only one. That was why I protected her! She hated me, but I would have changed that. I can change all people to my pattern.' His voice had become loud under the surge of rhetoric. Several of the legionnaires stirred in their sleep

Monclaire said: 'Do you realize that she is in the fort and, therefore, in danger of being killed by the Arabs?'

Pavani's words were pitched low again as he answered, 'Yes, I know that. And since I can't have her, perhaps it is as well for her to die.'

★   ★   ★

Pavani went back to one of the villas. It was her home. The place where she had lived.

He had ordered that it be left undisturbed during his absence and his orders had been obeyed. He stood in the middle of the tiny living room. It was in this room that he had found one of his men beating her. If he had arrived a few minutes later

184

she might have been dead.

With careful deliberation, he put back his head and sniffed. It was still there! A faint odour of perfume. It had endured through the tumultuous days since she had left the place and it remained to remind him. He went into her bedroom. Here, too, there was a pathetic effort to simulate normal comforts. The suite, provided by the French government, had been repainted a shade of pink. But it had not been foreseen that the unrelenting heat of Tutana would make that paint blister. On the dressing table he saw her toilet articles. He handled them carefully, reverently. There was a silver-backed hairbrush and comb with her initials engraved upon them. There was also a bowl of powder, and an almost used lipstick that bore the name of a New York store . . .

These were things she had touched and made her own. Once they had been part of the form of her living. Now a hundred miles of desert divided her from them. A hundred miles, plus a barrier of enraged Arabs.

Pavani dropped into a wicker chair and

thought. Human life? It was nothing when considered individually. People had to die some time. Against the whole span of human existence it did not matter whether they died at the age of eight or eighty. Whether they expired of senile decay or a bullet in the belly. But he wished that she had lived for him . . .

Now, he reminded himself, he must face his life's work alone. His life's work? What was that? Why had he dedicated himself to this violent struggle against any and all forms of authority? Why had his own people hounded him until he had been compelled to find a temporary refuge in the legion? The legion! The place where authority and obedience were at their highest level. It was in the nature of things that he should rebel against it and lead others into rebellion.

But he was avoiding the question. Why had he given himself to this fight? Why was it that he loathed all legal power? The reason was not difficult for him to recall. He was the son of a peasant. That was the root of it. His father, bound in semi-serfdom to a landlord in the Po Valley, had never thought about freedom, and so he was scarcely aware of his slavery. But that was not so of the son! No, the younger Pavani had rebelled.

When he was a child, other children had laughed at him because he was ugly. 'Your head is too big, Pavani . . . You have eyes like a forest wolf, Pavani . . . You are a dwarf, Pavani . . . ' They had refused to play with him. And even his parents had had little time to spare for their strange-looking offspring.

So he had been alone. And he had taught himself to read. With fierce intensity he had taught himself, with just a little help sometimes from the local priest. Then, when still a youth, a world had opened before him. He had read the doctrines of Proudhon and Bakunin. They showed him the truth. They showed him that no man need be dependent on another. That the natural state of life was one in which authority was absent or nearly absent. So men must fight to destroy authority. This was the revelation! This was the promise for the future! No more would people say to him: 'Pick it up

187

Pavani! Put it down, Pavani! Do it because I say so, Pavani.'

He had found he could write. Verse, in particular, had come easily from his pen. Violent verse which symbolised his beliefs. And much of it had been published in the extremist newspapers, of which Italy had many.

He had also found he could lead. Men forgot his appearance when they became aware of his knowledge and his ruthless strength. Ruthless . . . That was what he had been. What he would have to be. Probably, it would be safe for him to return to Italy now, for memories are short. So he would start there again. And he would show no mercy, for he had received none.

But if only she were with him! If only he could see her again . . .

He slept, with her perfume in his nostrils.

★   ★   ★

'Barrels of oil,' Monclaire said. 'I did not think about it at the time, but suddenly I realised that barrels of oil are stored next to this office.'

The legionnaires regarded him with mixed expressions. They were baffled, curious, or merely indifferent. And all were faintly resentful because it was barely night, and Monclaire had awakened them.

But Monclaire was talking briskly through the gloom. 'Then I thought to myself that oil burns! If we could reach those barrels, *mes amis*, we might be able to start a fire which would destroy every building in Tutana!'

The Polish legionnaire coughed. He said: 'But, *mon officier*, what good would that do us?' The Pole, although an experienced soldier, was not very bright. And Monclaire was compelled to be patient.

'The supplies for the march must be stored in one of the buildings near here. If we could start a fire which would destroy them — then there could be no escape for the Zephyrs.'

Rex scrambled to his feet. Here was a suggestion that made an instant appeal to his innate desire for action. 'It ought to be easy,' he said. 'With oil stored on the other side of the wall, we can't miss.'

Monclaire shook his head. 'It won't be easy. There will, on the contrary, be many difficulties.'

'There certainly will!' The clipped tones of Pete Havers came through the gathering darkness. He was adjusting his shoulder bandage as he spoke. 'For one thing, *capitaine*, are you sure that the barrels you saw *were* oil? The next building to this seems an unlikely storage place for the stuff.'

'I don't think so, Legionnaire. It is very probable that Pavani intends to burn the place himself when we leave tomorrow. The oil will by now be distributed all over Tutana. Certainly there will be plenty of it available . . . '

Several of them started to speak at once. Men who would never have thought of interrupting Monclaire under normal circumstances were now doing so with impunity. Monclaire did not mind. In fact, he welcomed the sudden interest. It was exactly what he wanted. His idea, he knew, was a desperate one. It could only succeed if it had the full co-operation of his men.

It was still Pete's voice, quiet and composed, which dominated the turbulence. He was less dubious now. 'I see the point, *capitaine*. The Zephyrs make the preparations, but we start the fire! There would certainly be a very good chance of destroying their stores — if we could get the flames started. But how are we to do it? We are prisoners, remember.'

Monclaire gestured towards the walls. 'Look,' he said. 'Examine the barrier which is between us and the oil barrels.'

Pete moved over with the others. There was not much light. But there was enough to see that, being an internal division, the wall was less robust than the others. It seemed to be composed of some form of fibre board — a light synthetic material. Pete tested it with the point of his clasp knife — one of the few possessions which the Zephyrs had overlooked. The stuff was hard, but it was brittle. Once pierced, it would probably crack easily. So it ought to be possible to break through.

But breaking through would be a long and noisy operation. The guards round the building would be sure to hear it. Pete voiced this difficulty.

'I know,' Monclaire said. 'But there must be some way of getting through without making too much noise.'

They became silent.

Then Pete laughed. '*Capitaine*,' he said, 'I think there's a way.'

* * *

The guards round the building stiffened in astonishment. It was a clear and musical sound that came from within. It was a song!

They consulted together. Then one of the Zephyrs went into the building. He released the safety catch of his Lebel before unlocking the prison door.

The brute paused, baffled. He saw a tall legionnaire, the American, standing in the middle of the floor, his head thrown back and his mouth wide open. The American was putting his soul into the lyrics.

'*This lovely rose will be a bond between us,*

Of sweet endeavour lasting through the years . . .'

The others were listening appreciatively, sitting in a half circle. None of them paid any attention to the guard.

The Zephyr glared at them suspiciously. He entered the room. He walked slowly round. Save for the singing, nothing unusual was happening. He counted the prisoners, marking each numeral on his fingers. Then he counted again. All of them were there: one of them singing, the others listening. After another careful look at the place he went out, relocking the door.

At the same time, the solo ceased on a note of vibrant ecstasy. There was a moment of quiet. Then all of them began singing at once. It was a weird and unmusical chorus. But they seemed to be enjoying it, for the volume was generous.

The Zephyr shook his head at his comrades. He was one of the less distinguished Germans. 'That the warm rhythm is,' he explained seriously. 'They try their spirits to keep up. They are mad.'

The others agreed that the legionnaires were quite clearly mad.

★　★　★

When the chorus was going well, Pete and Monclaire withdrew their vocal contributions. They moved over to the internal wall and kneeled at its base. One other knife had survived the fumbling Zephyr search. That had been loaned to Monclaire. Together they pressed the blades into the material. It needed more pressure than they had expected, but they dare not use too much strength in case the steel snapped. At points about two feet apart and some six inches above the floor, they levered and prodded. The stuff was thick, too. After five minutes neither of them had made a complete penetration.

And by this time the singing was becoming fainter. But it was essential to maintain the maximum amount of sound in case the partition split suddenly.

Rex came over. His voice was hoarse. 'We just can't keep going much longer,' he said. 'My choir needs a rest.'

Pete turned a sweating face to him. 'Try breaking it up a bit,' he suggested. 'Don't all sing at once. Half of you take a rest for a couple of minutes, then let the other half have a breather. Make a part song of it!'

'Okay, I'll do that. But lay off that chiselling while I get the troupe organised.'

Pete and Monclaire put down their knives. They tried to relax. But their nerves were strained. They knew that there was every chance of the guards making another inspection. And they might notice the deep marks on the wall, for moonlight was streaming in.

Presently the reorganised chorus struck up. They picked up their knives. And at that moment the door opened. Pavani was there. Automatically, the song faded away. But it had masked the turning of the lock.

He blinked curiously about him. Then he switched on an electric torch. The beam played on the now silent singers. Pavani said: 'Perhaps you will tell me what you are doing? I hope you are not attempting anything foolish.'

He was about to flash the light round the rest of the room. But Rex stopped him. Rex said in his indescribably bad French: 'Why can't you leave us alone?

Can't we try to cheer ourselves up without you coming in to stop us?'

Pavani turned the beam full on Rex's face. Rex had to lower his eyes.

'If you are trying to make the best of matters, then I am happy. I have told your captain that I hope for friendly co-operation from you all. But that noise you have been making — it jars! It is terrible! It is not music at all!'

Rex looked downcast. 'We'll improve.'

'If you are planning similar diversions while we are on the march, I can only say that I hope so . . .'

He flashed the torch round the room. The big circle of light moved along the partition. The figure of Legionnaire Pete Havers lay full length, eyes half closed, shoulders propped against the base of it. Pete yawned. He said:

'If you're complaining about the row, Pavani, I fully agree with you. I'm trying to get some sleep . . .'

The voice of Monclaire emerged from the gloom. '*Mais oui*. But if they are enjoying themselves, then let them sing on.'

The torch was directed at Monclaire. He was revealed to be sitting in very correct isolation in a far corner. There was an expression of amused tolerance on his unshaven face.

Pavani's tones became conciliatory. 'My dear *capitaine*! Who am I to interfere? If you do not object to this extraordinary performance, then it must continue.'

'A song is always good for morale,' Monclaire suggested.

'A song, yes. But . . . ' Pavani shrugged. He hesitated. Then he went out.

There was a painful pause, broken only by heavy breathing. Pete got up from his prone position, revealing once more the scars on the wall. He said: 'It seems our venture has official blessing, so let's make the most of it.'

Again the room reverberated to the ghastly cacophony. And again Pete and Monclaire worked with their clasp knives. Pete's knife was the first to penetrate. He felt the blade slide through the fibre and stop at the hilt. The next moment Monclaire's blade was through. Together, they twisted the hafts. There was a splintering report which the songsters' efforts only partly drowned. But they did not pause. They could see two long vertical cracks. They pushed with their hands against the bottom of the fibre. There was another report, but not quite so loud, and a piece of the wall fell into the adjoining building.

Sensing success, the singers stopped again.

'Keep going,' Pete hissed. 'Fade out gradually. Try to make it sound as if you're tired.'

The hole was large enough for a man to crawl through without difficulty. Monclaire was already half through it. Pete heard him give an exclamation of pleasure. '*Ah bon!* It is perfect!'

He disappeared. Pete crawled after him. He found himself in a larger room than the one he had just left. In the centre were four large barrels. Pete now had no doubts about what they contained. The faint and not unpleasant colour could only be oil. Probably it was oil that had been drawn off from the lines for testing.

There was also another sickly smell. It could not be identified.

There were two windows, both well above eye level, so there was no danger of being observed from outside. And the windows here, unlike that in the office, were not barred. It seemed likely that this room had been used for miscellaneous clerical equipment, for several unopened boxes of stationery were piled in a corner.

Monclaire moved forward to look more carefully at the barrels. He stumbled and fell forward. Pete grabbed his elbow and helped him up. Monclaire rubbed a grazed shin. Then he said: 'There is something on the floor . . . it felt like . . . ' He bent down.

Pete heard him gasp. Then he swore. When he straightened his face was pale in the moonlight. Monclaire said: 'You have some matches, *oui*?'

Pete pulled a box from his tunic pocket. Shading the light with his hands, he struck one and looked at the floor — and felt a sudden desire to vomit. He turned away and let the match fall. Monclaire stamped it out.

The body of a legionnaire was stretched out there. Or more accurately, the clothed skeleton of one, for the rats had visited him. His bones were picked clean where they showed beneath the tatters of his uniform. Pete's voice shook as he said: 'He — he must have been killed during the mutiny?'

'*Oui*. He was a corporal. He has been here more than two weeks . . . they must have known . . . but they would not bother to bury him. *Non!* They preferred to let the rats do their work . . . '

Pete had to force himself to strike another match. He bent over the repulsive remains, holding his breath against the sickly smell, which had been noticeable when they first entered. Full leather equipment was still hanging loosely on the bones. He pulled open the ammunition pouches. There were clips of nearly fifty rounds of .300 Lebel cartridges there. He cast his eyes further. Then he saw what he had been hoping to see.

It was a rifle.

The Lebel lay a yard from the dead legionnaire, partly concealed by an empty packing case. Pete picked it up. He fondled it. The feel of the cool blue steel was like the touch of a friend. He whipped back the bolt. An expended cartridge flew sideways out of the breech. He probed with his fingers and knew that the magazine was charged.

He said to Monclaire: 'You had better take this, *mon capitaine*. It may be useful.'

'*Non*, you keep it. You will be a better marksman than I, for you use a rifle every day.'

They shuffled away from the body after Pete had removed the ammunition pouches.

The singing from the other room was becoming fainter. The legionnaires were making a convincing imitation of men who were about to fall asleep.

They made a careful examination of the rest of the floor in the hope of finding more weapons, but there were none. Obviously, the room had been defended by that one man — and his Lebel had been overlooked.

It was as they were completing a circuit of the place that Pete saw the door. It was directly opposite the wall by which they had entered. He turned the handle carefully. He pulled very slowly. It opened inwards. There was no sound from it. A breath of cold wind blew in their faces.

And they saw the Zephyr. He had his back to them and he was a bare few inches away. He was a tall, powerful man — far more so than either Pete or Monclaire. And he was leaning slightly forward on the barrel of his rifle. He was completely unaware of their presence.

Pete was about to move on him, but Monclaire waved him away. Pete knew why. He knew that his shoulder wound had cost him strength. Monclaire was in a better condition to handle this.

And Monclaire handled it well. He did two things at the same time: he linked his hands round the Zephyr's forehead and pulled back, and he pushed a knee into the small of the Zephyr's back and pulled. The man swayed. He produced a soft coughing sound from the back of his throat. His rifle fell from his grasp, but Pete caught it before it touched the ground. Then there was a sound like the snapping of a dry twig.

His backbone had snapped at a lower vertebra. The almost clinical killing had taken less than ten seconds. Monclaire glanced quickly through the open door. Then he closed it as Pete pulled the body inside.

'It is quiet,' Monclaire said. 'Nobody saw. Get the others in here, then we will start, *mon ami* . . . we will make things warm in Tutana . . . '

Rex and his 'choir' were waiting anxiously. They had given up all pretence of singing now. They clustered eagerly round Pete.

'Are you okay?' Rex asked. 'Can we burn this place?'

'We can certainly burn this building,' Pete told them. 'And we've a fair chance of starting fires in some of the others, too . . . ' In a few moments he outlined what had happened. Then he led them back through the hole.

Monclaire had not wasted time. He had turned the bung taps at the base of the barrels and already thick oil was spreading over the stone floor. He looked almost happy. 'Your matches,' he said to Pete. Pete handed over the box. They moved towards the outer door.

Monclaire said: 'I am going to throw a match. The whole floor will be alight almost instantly, so there must be no hesitation about getting out. Understand?'

Seven faces, all expressing various degrees of tension, made it clear that they understood.

Monclaire added: 'There will, I think, be oil in all the buildings. But we must try to find the one where the Zephyr stores are stacked. Unless we destroy those, then there will be nothing to stop them marching according to plan. So, *mes amis*, that is our next operational objective — find and fire the stores. *Bonne chance*!'

He struck a match, then tossed it into the deepening pool of oil. There was a hollow, puffing sound like a giant taking a breath. Then the floor was a bed of white fire.

Flames were clinging to their boots as they burst out into the open.

10

The Mules

Monclaire was the last to emerge. He closed the door behind him, hoping that the discovery of the fire would thus be delayed by a few precious seconds. They must, he knew, get well clear of that building before the Zephyrs started rushing towards it. But he was at a disadvantage. He had had no opportunity to study the topography of Tutana and neither had the others. They would be working blind, trusting to instinct and common sense.

The legionnaires were huddled under the shadow of the wall — a wall which was already becoming warm from the heat within. Monclaire peered carefully around. There was a small, shack-like structure opposite, less than twenty yards away. He pointed towards it. They broke into a run. Fortunately, their boots made little noise. There had been no attempt to pave any part of Tutana and the ground was a mixture of soft soil and sand.

They reached the far side of the shack without seeing a sentry. They were panting more because of emotional stress than physical effort as they remustered. Monclaire peeped round the angle of the building, trying to get a general conception of the layout of the settlement. The place, it seemed, consisted of one main street and little else. On the other side and to his right he made out the outline of a villa. He also discerned the vague hulks of other buildings. But beyond that, he could see nothing.

'That equipment,' he muttered. 'It must be stored somewhere!'

Pete said: 'We saw the Zephyr camp when we arrived. It's outside the village. Could the equipment be there?'

'No, I think not. The Zephyrs live in tents. There would not be enough room. Remember that many tons of food would have to be carried to feed four hundred men on such a march. It will be assembled in one of the buildings.'

Rex, who had taken over the second

rifle, edged forward. 'Tons of food?' he queried.

'*Mais oui*. It must be so.'

'Then I guess they must have some sort of transport for it.'

'But of course. They will have mules — mules are always used when roads are being built, so there will be many of them in this area.'

Rex suddenly became excited. 'Then we don't need to hunt for the equipment! How about finding the mules?'

Monclaire and Pete then realised what the American was getting at. If they could locate the mules and drive them out into the desert, the Zephyrs would be without any means of carrying their stores, so the march would be impossible. As a plan, it could be quite as effective as destroying the stores themselves. And it would probably be easier to put into operation, for mules have a habit of revealing their presence, and they were not likely to be very well guarded.

Monclaire put a spontaneous hand on Rex's shoulder. He breathed: '*Merci, legionnaire*.'

At that moment they sniffed the first taint of smoke in the air, and they heard a series of light thuds. Then the light became swathed in a faint red glow. The fire was taking hold. It seemed that part of the roof had fallen in.

From somewhere near the office a Zephyr shouted. His voice was loud with surprise and anxiety. There were answering shouts. The legionnaires pressed against the shack as they heard feet running down the street towards the blaze. But for the moment they were in little danger. The Zephyrs' attention would be concentrated entirely on the outbreak.

Monclaire said: 'I think we have about a minute before they find that we have gone — follow me!'

Keeping behind the buildings, they moved parallel with the road and away from the fire. Monclaire was confident that he could find the mules without difficulty. Logically, they would be stabled or penned in at a point near the road head. And he knew where the road head was. It was to the north.

The red glow did not fade as they put

distance between themselves and the flames; it got brighter. The adjoining buildings must have caught alight.

They came upon the road head unexpectedly. It commenced at the fringe of Tutana. And since work on it had only been going on for a few weeks before the mutiny, it appeared as no more than a ribbon of rubble. Strewn around were the tools of slavery — the shovels and picks and barrows. Some of the Zephyrs must have been working there when the signal came to revolt.

Monclaire put up a hand and they stopped. They gazed around them. And as they did so they heard a burst of fresh shouting from behind them. It was faint because of the distance, but its meaning was clear. Their escape had been discovered.

Rex fingered his Lebel. 'Maybe I'd better go back and hold them off when they come this way,' he suggested.

Monclaire smiled. He shook his head. '*Non*, we will worry about the Zephyrs when we have driven the mules away — but first we must find them.'

209

The Pole saw them first. He pointed to a barely discernible, box-like outline. It was about two hundred yards away and to the east of the road. Then they heard a distinct stamping of hooves and a nervous neigh.

Pete said: 'They're penned into a compound. That makes it easier.'

'But it will not be too easy,' Monclaire warned. 'There will be at least one guard there. I hope he is too interested in the fire to see us. Move quietly, *mes amis*.' He looked at Pete and Rex, then added: 'Do not shoot unless you must.'

Under Monclaire's orders they spread out, approaching the compound from a point facing the settlement. The mules were panicking. That fact became apparent as they eased nearer. The stamping of hooves was loud and continuous. So was the neighing.

Pete whispered to Monclaire: 'It's the fire. It makes all anmials nervous. They'll stampede of their own accord.'

Monclaire was about to make some comment, but instead he pointed in front of him. They followed the direction of his finger and they saw the Zephyr sentry. He had been gazing towards the flames. *Had been* . . . He had been concealed by a patch of shadow thrown by one of the distant buildings. *Had* been . . .

Now he was stepping out of that shadow and turning towards them, as if suddenly aware of a hostile presence. He made a movement to unsling his rifle as he saw the line of legionnaires. But he did not do so. His slab-like features broke into a welcoming smile as Pete said casually, in a debased French: 'The prisoners have tried to escape, but there is no need to worry. We have caught them all.'

The Zephyr had a yellow-brown skin. He was probably a Mongolian. He asked: 'Did they start the fire?'

'They did,' Pete said. 'And they will pay for it. Pavani knows how to deal with such swine.'

The line was moving steadily on the Zephyr. Still he had not recognized them in the red half-light. And he did not recognize them until they were less than six feet away. Then it was too late to resist and too late to run.

Rex crouched slightly. He took an easy forward jump. As he landed, he reversed his rifle, pulling the barrel towards him and pushing the butt upwards in an arc. The wood crashed against the under part of the Zephyr's jaw. He remained standing for a fraction of a second while the lower half of his face seemed to slip sideways. Then he toppled slowly backwards and lay still, his slit eyes half open and gazing blankly up at the sky.

Rex gave Pete a strained smile. 'That was nice teamwork,' he said.

Monclaire interrupted before Pete could answer. He was holding the guard's rifle. 'I think we are lucky,' he said. 'There's no sign of other guards here. Now, *mes legionnaires*, we must find the gate of the compound . . .'

The compound was a simple, but effective, construction. It consisted of wood piles driven deep into the ground and linked by strands of thick wire. Within it, they could see some fifty or sixty excited beasts. They were rearing and kicking as they succumbed to an age-old fear of fire.

Pete found the gate. It was a crude

affair on leather hinges and secured by a loose loop. He dragged it open while the others flattened themselves against the wire, waiting for the stampede.

But it did not come. Not immediately. The mules reacted with the perversity of their breed: they ignored the wide opening while obviously seeking means of escape. They pressed against the wire, but paid no attention to the place where the wire had been removed.

Monclaire said: 'We will have to go in and drive them out . . . '

'All of us would probably be kicked to death if we did,' Pete hissed. 'If we can get just one of them through the gate the others will follow . . . '

He acted on his own suggestion. A single animal was standing near him, forelegs wide apart. Its head was hanging over the wire. Pete gripped its long ears and pulled it towards the opening. The mule bared its teeth and whinnied a protest. After a few reluctant steps it stopped. Rex slapped its quarters. The startled animal bucked. Then it charged out of the gate, paused, then galloped away from the town and towards the northern desert.

The result of this involuntary leadership was dramatic. The other mules made a concerted rush for the opening. The wire sagged and parts of it snapped as they, too, found freedom and made for the open wastes.

The legionnaires were still and silent for several moments after the last of the hoofbeats had faded. Then Rex said: 'We've fixed the Zephyrs. There'll be no march for the coast now, I guess. But what about us? If we stay around here the Zephyrs will butcher us . . . Maybe we ought to follow the mules.'

Pete said dryly: 'The mules will be able to fend for themselves. They'll find water and they'll eat cactus. We wouldn't be able to do that. If we go into the desert as we are now, we'll die in a few days.'

'And if we stick around this place we'll die in a few minutes,' Rex pointed out. And that ended the brief conference. They all looked at Monclaire for a decision.

Monclaire was staring towards the burning buildings. Flames now licked high into the sky, and even from this distance they could feel the heat from them. It was obvious that all the buildings in the vicinity of the office must have caught fire. It would be hours before they burned themselves out.

Because Monclaire did not speak, Pete asked: 'What do we do, *capitaine*?'

There was a feeling of anti-climax among them. They had achieved so much. The Zephyrs were trapped. They might be able to hold out in Tutana for weeks or months, but ultimately they would have to surrender. But, so far as the legionnaires themselves were concerned, their position was essentially the same. In effect, they were still prisoners. There was death in the desert. There was death in Tutana. Their only freedom, it seemed, was a choice between two ways of dying.

However, Monclaire focused their minds on a vital point — a point which they had forgotten. 'Pavani's still alive,' he said, articulating each word carefully. 'And we are armed. Between us we have three rifles. We can kill Pavani. We must kill Pavani, even as we would seek out and slay a mad dog.'

Rex said: 'I don't get it. There's no escape for him now. He'll be captured when the legion retake this place and . . . '

'Perhaps, Legionnaire. Perhaps. But what will he do in the meantime? He may raid more Arab villages — this time to get mules in an effort to replace those he has lost. And he will be immune from attack. Even if the High Command can assemble sufficient forces, they would not assault Tutana it they did so; Pavani would destroy the oil lines. He is trapped, *mon ami*, but he can still cause terrible harm.

'You remember that we tried to kill him before? Why? Because we knew that without his leadership the Zephyrs would be helpless. They are evil men, but they have the minds of infants. *Oui*, the same is true now. If . . . if we could kill Pavani, I think I might be able to persuade the Zephyrs to surrender.'

'Those vandals,' Pete exclaimed. 'Persuade them to surrender? They'd pull you to pieces before you got a couple of words out.'

'I think not,' Monclaire said, smoothly. 'It would be necessary to kill Pavani and

216

then hide for a few hours so as to give them time to realise the hopelessness of their position. If their first anger had died away, I think they would listen to me. Now I want . . . '

Rex interrupted. He was waving his rifle in the direction of the village. 'The meeting's over,' he shouted. 'The Zephyrs are coming — and they've seen us . . . '

11

Keyboard Crisis

The Zephyrs were silhouetted against the background of the flames, advancing shoulder-to-shoulder in a single, long line. They were about three hundred yards from the legionnaires and bearing directly upon them.

Pete said: 'It looks like the whole battalion . . . we've got to move rather fast, I fancy.'

Monclaire smiled faintly at the typical English understatement. Then he said to Rex: 'You are wrong. We have not been seen.'

'But they must be able to see us if we can see them!'

'*Non.* They have the light behind them. We have a background of darkness. We are quite invisible and we are in no immediate danger. We will just move away quietly along the line of the road and we will halt when they halt. *Avant!*'

Rex was not satisfied. As they withdrew he said: 'If they haven't seen us, why are they coming straight for us?'

'*Tiens!* Because they are making an end-to-end sweep of the town, and we, Legionnaire, are at one end of it. I think we will hear something interesting from them in a few seconds.'

Pete said: 'You mean when they discover that the mules have gone?'

'Precisely. At the moment we have been no more than a nuisance to the Zephyrs. The fire that we started is not likely to have worried them much, and they will be confident of recapturing us — they'll know that we cannot get far without food and water. But their outlook will change when they see the empty compound.'

With Monclaire in the rear, they retreated along the rubble of the road-head. They had been moving thus for about a minute when they heard the distant babble of voices. They stopped and looked back. The Zephyrs had broken their extended order and were rushing towards the compound. Some of them were forming into groups. One group doubled back towards the village — probably to report to Pavani.

Monclaire drew their attention to this. And he said: 'They will wait for Pavani to arrive. So will we. And when we see him we will shoot. It ought to be easy to identify him.'

'But not so easy to hit him at this range,' Pete said. 'He is not likely to stand still and the others will be moving about, too.'

'*Oui*, it will be difficult — but we may never get another chance.'

Then Pavani arrived. They knew he had arrived at the compound because of the sudden surge of Zephyrs towards him. No other figure in Tutana would attract so much attention. They waited for the moment when he would appear from out of the shouting, gesticulating mob — for the moment when Monclaire, Pete and Rex could draw a bead on him through the sights of their Lebels. They watched the mob move round the outside of the compound. They watched it go into the compound. They watched it emerge again. But they did not catch even a glimpse of Pavani.

Pete wiped his brow with his sleeve. 'He's keeping in the middle of them,' he said. 'It's almost as if he has guessed . . . '

'I think he *has* guessed,' Monclaire murmured. 'He won't know where we are, but he will know that we have the rifles, for they'll have found the sentries. *Dieu*! That man! Always he is one move ahead of us!'

'Not quite always,' Pete corrected. 'We've had a few successes tonight.'

'*Attendre*! Something is happening!'

Something was indeed happening. Most of the Zephyrs had reformed their single line and were again moving forward: a small group — obviously surrounding Pavani — and retreating into the village and out of sight.

Monclaire lowered his Lebel. They once more fell back along the road. Monclaire's forehead was furrowed with perplexity. He had felt sure that Pavani would not order his men to continue the hunt in the open desert. In darkness it would be a futile task. Then why were the Zephyrs continuing their sweep so far out of Tutana? There was only one answer. There must be some other building, some other place of importance, along this road. But what was it? What could it be which was placed well beyond the limits of the village?

Then they saw it: a small, square concrete building which looked oddly white against the sand. And on top of it they saw a towering steel radio mast.

* * *

Corporal Annicka Loto, the wireless operator, was a man of uncertain nationality who had found himself in an uncertain position. His skin suggested a strong Oriental strain. But his round eyes gave the impression of an Occidental background. His black and woolly hair did more than hint at African antecedents.

He had been posted to Tutana a few weeks before the mutiny. He had not liked the posting. Corporal Loto had quailed at the sight of the Zephyrs and spent as much time as possible in the security of his radio room. He was glad that his duties did not require him to help guard the penal battalion. Loto was a gifted man in the field of wireless telegraphy, but he was no hero. And, because he was no hero, he had willingly agreed to carry on with his duties when the Zephyrs had burst into his room on that terrible morning.

At first, he had been glad to take orders from Pavani. It seemed a cheap price to pay in exchange for his life. But later he had not been so sure. He was expected to listen in to all messages between legion garrisons and send immediate transcriptions to Pavani. That meant that he dare not sleep, save in short snatches, which was exhausting. His spirits had been getting steadily lower.

Then, earlier that evening, a new and chilling thought had occurred to him. The sentry outside had told him of the impending march.

'We start in the morning,' the Zephyr had said. 'You'll get all the rest you need then!'

You'll get all the rest you need . . .

Loto had repeated the words to himself many times. He had tried to detect the inner meaning. Then, to his horror, it became clear to him. When they left Tutana the Zephyrs would have no need for the skilled services of Corporal Loto! They would not take him with them. Why should they? He was not a Zephyr. He was the only survivor of the legion guards. They would kill him!

As he sat hunched over his valves and dials, Loto felt that he would vomit. If only he could get out! Run away. Run anywhere. But there was always a sentry outside the radio station. He would be shot before he covered a dozen paces.

When would they kill him? Perhaps they would not wait until the morning. It could be this very night. He looked desperately out of the barred window. He saw the red glow in the sky. It had been there for an hour, but he had not bothered about it, except to conclude that the Zephyrs were destroying the village before leaving. If only those windows had not been barred . . . But the door was the only way out. And the sentry was there.

'I'm going to die,' Loto croaked to himself, his tones suggesting that such an event was in contradiction to the laws of nature. 'I wish they'd give me a little longer. I wish they'd wait until morning! But I don't think they will . . . I think they'll come now . . .'

He heard the stamp of many feet outside. He heard voices — rough, merciless voices. He forced himself out of his swivel chair and reeled to the window. God! They had sent the whole Zephyr battalion to murder him! There were hundreds of them out there! Loto braced himself against the wall so as to ease the burden on his jellied legs. He stared at the door. He heard someone speak to the sentry and the sentry answer. The knob turned. The door opened. An enormous Zephyr stood there, looking round. He gave Loto only a brief glance. Then he went out, slamming the door.

For a time, Loto could not fully realise that he was still alive. He staggered to the door, opening it with trembling fingers. He peeped through a narrow aperture. The cold night wind met his sweating face. Everything was normal.

No — it wasn't normal! There were

now three sentries outside the building instead of the usual one. They were making sure he did not escape!

Loto got back to his chair. His skin was glistening. His eyes were swimmmg. He sank his head into his hands and drifted into a semi-swoon.

★   ★   ★

Pete peered over the top of the sand dune. Then he said softly: 'They are going away — but they're leaving a couple of extra sentries.'

Monclaire edged forward and looked cautiously. He saw the Zephyrs walking back to the village. He saw, a bare thirty yards away, the door of the radio station and the three guards outside it. Then he again took cover, motioning Pete to do the same. He looked excited. The seven men huddled close to him as he spoke in a quick whisper.

'*Mes amis*, we will try to seize the radio station! I want to get a message to the fort. Such a message might convince the Arabs of what has been happening

— I do not say it will, but it might, for if Gina learns that the column has been destroyed he will certainly show the Arabs the signal. Unless the Arabs are fools, they will hesitate to go on with their plan to attack the fort. They will at least seek confirmation.'

There was an uneasy movement among the legionnaires. Pete said: 'How are we going to deal with the sentries? We are close enough to the village for any shooting to be heard.'

'I know, Legionnaire — that is why the Zephyrs are content with a guard of three. And, in any case, they do not know we are in this area. They will naturally think we have retired as far as we can into the desert.' Monclaire paused, then added: 'I think we can handle the sentries, and I think we can do it without any noise. Listen to me carefully . . . '

★   ★   ★

The three Zephyrs were disgruntled. They objected strongly to standing outside the radio station. When told to do so they had argued fiercely. They had only submitted when the name of Pavani was mentioned. It was better to spend a night in the cold than to cross such a man as he.

After half an hour they had ceased grumbling to each other. They were leaning against the wall, almost asleep, when they heard the thud of approaching feet on the rubble of the road. They fingered their Lebels, then detached themselves from the building. The Zephyrs were not unduly alarmed, for the sound came from the direction of Tutana, and there was no attempt to disguise it. Presently, they saw the dim outline of four men against the red sky. The Zephyrs raised their rifles and challenged them. One of the four stepped forward.

'Pavani has sent us,' he said. 'We have to share the guard with you.'

A Zephyr said: 'Does he not think there are enough of us out here?'

'He fears the legionnaires may try to seize the radio station.'

'The legionnaires will not be anywhere near this place, comrade. They will be far out in the desert.'

228

'That's what we think. And if the scum do not die of thirst the Arabs will surely kill them. But Pavani is taking no risks.'

The Zephyrs grounded their Lebels and relaxed. Their spokesman said casually: 'What are your names? We cannot see . . . '

It was at that moment that he felt fingers encircle his throat from behind. He felt a cruel, inhuman pressure against his windpipe. He could not draw air into his lungs and neither could he breathe it out. His chest felt as if it was splitting down the middle and drums were beating in his head.

The Zephyr dropped his rifle. He tried to grope over his shoulders. But his hands had suddenly become heavy — as if great weights had been hung on them. He wondered why the two others did not help him. But in the second before the final blackness he saw why. He saw that they, too, were writhing in the grip of strangling fingers. And the men who said they had come to join the guard? They were watching.

Just watching . . .

*   *   *

Again, the door opened. Again, Corporal Loto prepared to meet his end. He raised a head that rolled loosely on his shoulders, like that of a newborn child. He focused his wet eyes on the men who stood before him: filthy, unshaven, sweating, desperate men.

But they did not look like Zephyrs. There was something different about them. One of them was in the uniform of a captain — and he wore it as if it belonged to him.

Loto heard the captain say: 'Are you the radio operator?'

He managed a wild nod.

'Then I have a message for immediate transmission. Hurry, man, look alive! It is from Captain Monclaire. It is to the acting commander, Fort Valeau . . . '

Loto put a twitching finger on his Morse key.

12

Blood Security

Lieutenant Gina had been a social success. It had been a magnificent evening that he had spent with Rene D'Aplis. They had dined well and this time there had been no suggestive leer on the face of the orderly. Throughout the meal they had talked fluently and easily to each other. It had been the same afterwards, when they sat facing each other in deep leather chairs.

What was the reason for this sudden transformation, which contrasted so greatly with the previous evening? It was quite simple. Gina had forgotten Professor Karlo. He had not tried to impress his beautiful guest. Gina had been Gina. And she had liked him for it. He had confided in her — even to the extent of revealing that he was afraid of Sergeant Zatov.

She had understood. She had been remarkably sympathetic. And she gave

Gina a new line of thought when she said: 'I think Sergeant Zatov is a lonely man, for he has lost his country and his friends, and his career as a Russian officer. He sees himself as a failure, yet he knows he has a spark of greatness in him. Perhaps that is why he cannot resist dominating young men like you, who have everything before them. But he intends no serious harm . . . he is not a spiteful man nor a mean one. I can tell . . . '

Those words had made a big impression on Gina. And now the evening was almost over. It was after midnight and she was about to go. She said: 'Thank you, Lieutenaut Gina. Tonight I have almost forgotten everything I have been through and — and everything I have lost. There is just one thing I must ask you, and I hope you won't think me ungrateful.'

'I'm sure I won't think anything of the sort, madame. What is it?'

'When do you think I'll be able to start for home? It's the memories of Morocco . . . I can forget them for a few hours. But I know they'll return. I do want to get out of the place.'

Gina felt a twinge of disappointment, but he did not show it. 'It depends on Monclaire. He will be back soon.'

'But those Arabs? They are very suspicious. Suppose Monclaire does not capture any Zephyrs? They may not believe that he has been after the mutineers.'

Gina laughed confidently. 'Monclaire will do what he set out to do. He is one of the best tacticians in the legion. He'll find that mob of Zephyrs and he'll get Pavani. Either he will kill them or capture them. Then the mutiny will collapse. I know — for I know Monclaire.'

She was about to answer when the door was flung open. It was Sergeant Zatov, holding a square of paper. And — most incredibly — the hand that held it was shaking. He ignored Rene. He gave Gina a perfunctory salute. Then he handed over the paper.

'Message from Captain Monclaire, *mon officier*!'

The first time he read it, Gina collected only a few confused and frightening impressions. He had to read it again before the meaning became clear. Even then he doubted whether it was genuine until he saw Monclaire's personal cipher number quoted at the top.

' . . . COLUMN TRAPPED BY ZEPH-YRS AT HAGAL. SEVEN SURVIVORS AND SELF TAKEN TO TUTANA. HAVE ESCAPED AND MADE ZEPHYR MARCH IMPOSSIBLE BY DRIVING AWAY TRANSPORT MULES. NOW HOLD RADIO STATION. FOOD AND WATER HERE. WILL FIGHT ON FROM HERE TO LAST MAN. MAY YET MANAGE TO KILL PAVANI. SHOW ARABS THIS MESSAGE. IT MAY CONVINCE THEM. *AU REVOIR*. MONCLAIRE.'

When Gina first tried to speak, only a choking sob emerged. He gazed wildly at Zatov. The Russian looked gaunt, and the fire had faded from his eyes.

With a great effort Gina said: 'Of course . . . there's nothing we can do. Nothing at all!' He did not notice that Rene had removed the message from his limp fingers.

Zatov crossed to the window and closed it. A shiver went through his massive frame. It was not caused by the chill of the night.

He spent a long and silent minute staring at his own reflection in the glass. Then he turned again to Gina. 'Our first duty is to try to remove the menace to the fort,' he said in a voice that no longer boomed. 'We must ask the headmen to meet us at once. We must do as Captain Monclaire says, and show them his message.'

'I don't think they will believe it, Zatov. They will think is a trick. And in any case, I doubt whether any of them can read French.'

'We must try to persuade them, *mon officier*. If we do not, they will surely attack and we cannot hold them off for long.'

'I know . . . Sergeant Zatov, we must do more than try to persuade them not to attack us. We must get them to help us. There are thousands of Arabs out there, and at least half of them have camels or horses. Don't you see? They could reach Tutana within thirty-six hours — perhaps less. They could see for themselves what has happened there . . . and they might be in time to save Monclaire and his men!'

'But the oil line, *mon officier*. Even if the Arabs agreed to do this, Pavani would order the oil lines to be destroyed. Monclaire would rather die than have that happen.'

Rene had been reading the message. Her face had become almost transparently white. She whispered: 'If I offered to go back to Tutana . . . if I offered myself as a hostage . . . do you think the Arabs would agree to go with me? Surely they would believe us then! I cannot offer them more than my life.'

Zatov put an immense hand on her shoulder. He said: 'You are a woman — but you have the heart of a man! Even my heroic people in the Ukraine would be glad to have you among them. But what you suggest is impossible.'

Gina nodded. 'Zatov is right. You are officially under the care of the French government. I could not think of letting you offer yourself as a hostage to the Arabs.'

She took a cigarette from a box on the table. When Gina had lit it, she said: 'Will I be safe if the Arabs attack this fort?'

They did not answer. She added: 'They said they would slay every legionnaire. Do you think they would spare me? I don't.'

Gina shrugged. 'We would protect you to the last man.'

'I am sure of that. But what would happen to me when the last man is dead? Listen . . . the Arabs seek vengeance against those who have attacked their villages. Already they half-believe what we have told them about the Zephyrs. They would have nothing to lose by going to Tutana to see for themselves. Those who are not mounted could stay here, still encircling the fort. They are human beings, aren't they? They must realise that we are not likely invent such a story as this. But if I offer to go with them, they can have no further doubts . . . '

Gina said: 'There's still the matter of the oil line.'

Zatov said: 'Let hell take the oil line! I was wrong to have reminded you of it. A thousand Arabs in a surprise attack could seize Tutana before the Zephyrs had a chance to start the explosions!' It was noticeable that Zatov's voice had regained some of its normal robust volume.

'We could not take a risk like that,' Gina ventured.

Rene said: 'There need be no risk to the oil lines — not if the Arabs can be persuaded to co-operate. This is what I suggest . . . '

* * *

Dawn was heavy upon the sky. The elder headman, who had been conferring with the others, said to Gina: 'We will do as you say. And the sergeant will come with us. But if we have been deceived, all of you will pay with your lives.'

13

The Return

Monclaire gazed slantwise through the shattered window. He saw the redness of the dying sun blending with the redness of the sand. He said: 'This is the second sunset we have seen from here.'

The Pole, who was a courageous pessimist, said: 'We will not see a third, *mon capitaine*.'

Monclaire did not answer. He looked upon the circle of Zephyrs who surrounded the radio station. More than three hundred of them . . . more than three quarters of their total strength. They had burrowed down into the sand, and from that cover they aimed sporadic shots through the window and through the door. The door was like a piece of latticework; it could not hang onto its hinges much longer.

Pete, who was standing beside Monclaire, said: 'They'll rush us as soon as it's dark.'

'I only regret that Pavani will not be leading them,' Monclaire answered.

Rex dabbed his chin with his sleeve. A ricochetted shot had grazed his skin. He murmured: 'Maybe those buzzards will get into this place . . . maybe they'll kill us. But that doesn't mean anything. It doesn't mean anything important.'

Monclaire said: 'I wish we could kill Pavani. The world would be a cleaner place without him . . . '

* * *

Pavani sat in the bedroom of the villa which had belonged to Rene D'Aplis. He breathed her perfume. It was becoming fainter with each day, like a memory that you strove to keep within the mind, but which was escaping gradually. Tomorrow, perhaps, the last of the fragrance would be gone. But he, Pavani, would be gone, too.

It was now sunset. He waited only for news that the radio station had been captured. Then he and his picked men would disappear from Tutana. They would be heavily laden, and they would have upon their backs all the supplies that a man could carry for a couple of miles. Then they would hide those supplies and march forward to the nearest Arab village, where they would seize all the available mules and camels. After that it would not be difficult. They would retrace their steps, put the supplies on the backs of the animals . . . then move north for the coast. If they ate and drank the absolute minimum they would survive the long trek.

Pavani had his regrets. He did not want to desert the men who were now surrounding the radio station. But he knew that he was compelled to do so. It would be easy to capture animals for a handful of men. But it would be impossible to do so for four hundred.

He stood up, paused, then went to the dressing table. He touched the toilet articles as if they were sacred things. He wondered which of them he should take with him . . .

He was still wondering when he heard the thud of running feet. He had a feeling of imminent crisis. A Zephyr burst into the room. His face was drenched in sweat. He was breathing in painful gasps. Pavani recognized him as one of the sentries from the outer perimeter of the town, one of his selected thirty. The Zephyr said: 'It's the woman . . . your woman . . . she is here!'

Pavani felt for the pistol in his holster. He would kill any man who joked with him on such a matter. The Zephyr saw his hand close on the butt and added quickly: 'It's the truth! She is here! Rene D'Aplis! We did not see her until she was almost upon us, for it's getting dark. But she is alone!'

'How did she get here?'

'She is on a horse. We questioned her, Pavani. She says she has come from Fort Valeau . . . she has come to see you . . .'

The man broke off as slow hoofbeats were heard from outside the villa. Then he added weakly: 'This is her . . . now you know I speak the truth!'

Pavani stood with his back to the dressing table. His head looked larger, more grotesque than usual. He was watching the door. Waiting for it to open. Waiting for her . . .

Then, quite suddenly, she was there.

She was standing in the doorway with a Zephyr on each side of her. She was slender, upright, beautiful. And faintly proud, like a flower which has survived the buffeting of a storm. There was no fear in her eyes as they met his.

He knew a desperate sense of expectation as she parted her lips to speak. Would her voice still have its richness and its hint of arrogance?

It had not changed. It was the voice he remembered which said to him: 'I have come back to you, Pavani.'

'You have come back to me! Why?'

She ignored the question. She said: 'Do you still want me? If you do, I am yours . . . willingly yours. But there is one condition I must make . . . '

Pavani did not move, save to glance at the Zephyrs. And to them he said: 'Get out!'

When they were alone he moved close to her. He extended his ungainly arms in a clumsy attempt to draw her to him. But she stepped back.

'Not now,' she said. 'First you must listen to me.'

'Yes — I will listen. How did you get

243

here? The captain told me you had got to the fort.'

'Monclaire spoke the truth. But two days ago I persuaded the lieutenant there to help me to escape from the place. The place is surrounded, but he managed to get me through the Arab lines. He even got me a horse . . . '

'Why did you want to leave Fort Valeau?'

'Why? Because I do not want to die! The Arabs were preparing to attack the place — they may have already done so. I realised that it was better to live . . . to live with you than to be killed at their hands.'

Lust was struggling with logic as he gazed at her. He said: 'What is the condition you make?'

She countered with another question. 'Do the legionnaires still hold the radio station?'

'They do. But it will be attacked tonight.'

'I see . . . If you want me to come to you willingly, you must let them go free and unharmed.'

'Let them go free! I cannot do that! And why should you ask it? They are nothing to you!'

'They are everything to me, Pavani. I am grateful to them. And you should be grateful, also.'

'I should be grateful to them . . . '

'But certainly. If they had not seized the radio station, if they had not sent a message revealing that their plight was hopeless, I would have stayed in the fort thinking that I was safe. I would have lost my life. And you would have lost me. You understand?'

He was very still for a long time. Then he nodded slowly. 'Yes, I understand. But if I let them go free, they will have little chance of survival. They will die of exposure or at the hands of the Arabs.'

'If you let them have supplies . . . '

'That would make no difference. It would only delay the end . . . ' He broke off because a new possibility was opening before him. If he were to spare their lives, he might as well take them with him. Monclaire's assistance would still be invaluable on the march. It would mean providing food and water for eight extra men, but that need not matter. As soon as the worst of the trek was over, he would

245

kill the legionnaires.

He heard her saying: 'It is my price if you want me. Will you pay it?'

Pavani said slowly: 'Yes, I will pay it. They will go free.' Again he tried to touch her, tried to draw her close to him. For a moment she looked afraid and she folded her arms protectively over the front of her dress.

'I want to see you give the order,' she said. 'I want to watch Monclaire and his men leave that place unharmed.'

He was breathing fast and his eyes were heavy. But he stood back. And he said: 'Very well . . . come with me.'

★ ★ ★

Monclaire could scarcely pronounce the words. 'It's Pavani!' he croaked. 'And there's a woman with him . . . *Dieu*! It's Rene D'Aplis!'

The legionnaires clustered round the window, peering cautiously. The darkness within the radio station was suddenly filled with muttered exclamations. They watched Pavani talking to the Zephyrs.

They saw that his words were being repeated along the ring.

Rex said: 'He's in range! This is our chance to shoot him!'

Monclaire put a restraining hand on Rex's elbow. 'Wait,' he said. 'The light is not good. You may kill her.'

Then they became rigid. They heard Pavani's voice and it was calling to them clearly. It said: 'You are free to go, legionnaires! You will not be harmed. But first I wish to speak alone with you, Captain Monclaire.'

There was a rumble of astonishment from the Zephyrs. All of them were looking at their leader. It was then that Rene put her hand beneath the front of her dress. She pulled out a pistol with a fluted barrel and pointed it upwards. There was a faint explosion, followed by a prolonged hiss. No one moved — not until a magnesium flare burst high in the sky, then floated slowly down, transforming the darkness into a harsh, artificial day. Then, and only then, did Pavani turn upon her. As he did so he uttered a short and satanic oath.

His arms were stretched out to her throat when she again fired the flare pistol. The explosive cartridge lodged in his chest. He put shaking hands over the wide wound. He looked down at the oozing blood. Then, when he realised what was about to happen, he screamed. It was an ordinary scream of ordinary human terror, such as he had heard when he had attacked the villages.

He was still screaming when the magnesium burst inside his body. He glowed pink, illuminated from within. Then he shrivelled into a ghastly ember. And as he did so, the Zephyrs heard the thunder of galloping horses, then saw the avenging Arabs sweeping down on them from behind the cover of the distant dunes. But they did not attempt to fight. They turned and tried to run.

Rene felt the surge of frightened, leaderless humanity about her. The pistol had fallen from her grasp and she was being forced out into the desert by the mob. She had to run with them. If she had attempted to remain still, she would have been knocked down and trampled to death.

Monclaire saw it happening. Pete saw it happening . . . And Monclaire said: 'Come — we still have work to do. We must get to her . . . ' They were moving away from the window when the Arabs came in view: a solid wall of a thousand mounted and blood-hungry men.

But not all of them were Arabs. A legionnaire was there: just one man in a blue uniform, who rode ahead of the others. But he was no ordinary man. He was a giant with a flaming red beard. And he had an Arab scimitar in his right hand.

Sergeant Zativ's horse ploughed a path through the retreating Zephyrs, and suddenly he was in the centre of them. His free hand stretched down and grasped Rene D'Aplis. Effortlessly, he held her under his arm as he turned the animal round and headed it towards where Captain Monclaire and his legionnaires were waiting.

★　★　★

She left them when the day was new, with an escort of forty legionnaires who had arrived for her from Dini Sadazi. But she could have travelled in equal safety without any escort, for the Arabs would have guided her and succoured her. The desert was at peace again.

Three men watched from the ramparts.

Rex said: 'She's going home — to my home . . . '

Pete said: 'I wish . . . but what's the use of wishing when you're a soldier?'

Zarov said: 'It is your only privilege, Legionnaire, so make use of it. I, too, am wishing.'

And standing at the open gates, Monclaire glanced at Gina and smiled. 'Don't be too depressed,' he said. 'I still think you are too young.'

Then he gave an order. The gates closed as Rene and her escort disappeared from sight over the shimmering horizon.

THE END